LUCY BY THE SEA

'Writing of this quality comes from a commitment to listening, from a perfect attunement to the human condition, from an attention to reality so exact that it goes beyond a skill and becomes a virtue' Hilary Mantel

'[Strout's] novels, intricately and painstakingly crafted, overlap and intertwine to create an instantly recognizable fictional landscape . . . you don't so much read a Strout novel as inhabit it' *Guardian*

'There is an insistent generosity in Strout's books, and a restraint that obscures the complexity of their construction' *Washington Post*

'A terrific writer' Zadie Smith

'Stunningly universal . . . with brilliant acuity, Strout has seized on the parallels between Lucy Barton's pervasive sense of alienation and the way the recent global crisis has exposed the helplessness felt by ordinary people everywhere' *Daily Telegraph*, 5 stars

'Strout's portrait of a divorced couple united by worry for their two grown daughters illuminates a refreshingly unexplored angle of Covid . . . They leap off the page along with their creator's salty wit and a phantom scent of hand sanitizer' *The New York Times*

'It's no secret that Elizabeth Strout is a stunning writer, but I still find myself amazed at the depth she brings to the world of her stories centred on Lucy Barton' Taylor Jenkins Reid, *Week*

'*Lucy by the Sea* holds a mirror up to everything we have been through recently. Not only reflecting disbelief, isolation and how different and at the same time similar we are to each other, but also what happens to human relationships when we can't be together. Superb' Claire Fuller, author of *Unsettled Ground*

'No novelist working today has Strout's extraordinary capacity for radical empathy, for seeing the essence of people beyond reductive categories, for uniting us without sentimentality. I didn't just love *Lucy by the Sea*; I needed it. May droves of readers come to feel enlarged, comforted and genuinely uplifted by Lucy's story' *Boston Globe*

'*Lucy by the Sea* is another Barton instalment that confronts the deep and familiar tangles of intimate relationships . . . Through this complex and isolating time, Lucy plumbs the nuances of human connection' *Time*

'Poised and moving . . . It is only in the steady hands of Strout, whose prose has an uncanny, plainspoken elegance, that you will want to relive those early months of wiping down groceries and social isolation . . . This is a slim, beautifully controlled book that bursts with emotion' *Vogue*

'An unflinching depiction of the ways we are all alone . . . Strout's most distinctive skill – the ability to render every character, big or small, with precision – is on full display . . . Lucy finds love in the novel, but Strout never looks away from the loneliness that is inherent in being human: "We all live with people – and places – and things that we have given great weight to. But we are all weightless in the end"' Sarah Collins, *Prospect*

'Strout captures the minutiae of recent years with insight and compassion' *i*, 40 Best Books to Read This Autumn

'After giving a beloved secondary character from her 2016 bestseller *My Name is Lucy Barton* his own standalone with last year's *Oh William!*, Strout returns to the source, packing her recently widowed heroine off to Maine from Manhattan during lockdown – and exploring, in her clean inimitable prose, no less than love, loneliness and what it means to be alive' *Entertainment Weekly*

BY ELIZABETH STROUT

Lucy by the Sea

Oh William!

Olive, Again

Anything is Possible

My Name is Lucy Barton

The Burgess Boys

Olive Kitteridge

Abide With Me

Amy and Isabelle

LUCY BY THE SEA

A Novel

ELIZABETH STROUT

PENGUIN BOOKS

PENGUIN BOOKS

UK | USA | Canada | Ireland | Australia
India | New Zealand | South Africa

Penguin Books is part of the Penguin Random House group of companies
whose addresses can be found at global.penguinrandomhouse.com.

First published in the United States of America by Random House,
an imprint and division of Penguin Random House LLC 2022
First published in Great Britain by Viking 2022
Published in Penguin Books 2023

001

Printed and bound in Great Britain by Clays Ltd, Elcograf S.p.A.

The authorized representative in the EEA is Penguin Random House Ireland,
Morrison Chambers, 32 Nassau Street, Dublin D02 YH68

A CIP catalogue record for this book is available from the British Library

ISBN: 978-0-241-60700-8

www.greenpenguin.co.uk

For my husband, Jim Tierney

And for my son-in-law, Will Flynt

With love and admiration for them both—

BOOK ONE

One

i

Like many others, I did not see it coming.

But William is a scientist, and he saw it coming; he saw it sooner than I did, is what I mean.

~

William is my first husband; we were married for twenty years and we have been divorced for about that long as well. We are friendly, I would see him intermittently; we both were living in New York City, where we came when we first married. But because my (second) husband had died and his (third) wife had left him, I had seen him more this past year.

About the time his third wife left him, William found out that he had a half-sister in Maine; he found it out on an ancestry website. He had always thought he was an only child, so this was a tremendous surprise for him, and he asked me to go up to Maine for two days with him to find her, and we did, but the woman—her name is Lois Bubar— Well, I met her but she did not want to meet William, and this made him feel very terrible. Also, on that trip to Maine we found out things about William's mother that absolutely dismayed him. They dismayed me as well.

His mother had come from unbelievable poverty, it turned out, even worse than the circumstances I had come from.

The point is that two months after our little trip to Maine, William asked me to go to Grand Cayman with him, which is where we had gone with his mother, Catherine, many, many years before, and when our girls were small we would go there with them and with her too. The day he came over to my apartment to ask me to go with him to Grand Cayman, he had shaved off his huge mustache and also cut his full white hair very short—and only later did I realize this must have been a result of Lois Bubar's not wanting to see him plus everything he had learned about his mother. He was seventy-one years old then, but he, kind of, I think, must have been plunged into some sort of midlife crisis, or older man crisis, with the loss of his much younger wife moving out and taking their ten-year-old daughter, and then his half-sister's not wanting to see him and his find-ing out that his mother had not been who he'd thought she had been.

So I did that: I went to Grand Cayman with him for three days in early October.

And it was odd, but nice. We had separate rooms, and we were kind to each other. William seemed more reticent than usual, and it was strange for me to see him without his mustache. But there were times when he threw his head back and really laughed. There was a politeness to us that was consistent; so it was a little strange, but nice.

But when we got back to New York, I missed him. And I missed David, my second husband, who had died.

I *really* missed them both, David especially. My apart-ment was so quiet!

~

I am a novelist and I had a book coming out that fall, and so after our trip to Grand Cayman I had a great deal of traveling to do around the country and I did it; this was in late October. I was also scheduled to go to Italy and Ger-many in the beginning of March, but in early December—

it was kind of odd—I just decided I was not going to go to those places. I never cancel book tours and the publishers were not happy, but I was not going to go. As March approached someone said, "Good thing you didn't go to Italy, they're having that virus." And that's when I noticed it. I think that was the first time. I did not really think about it ever coming to New York.

But William did.

ii

It turned out that the first week in March, William had called our daughters, Chrissy and Becka, and asked—begged—them to leave the city; they both lived in Brooklyn. "And don't tell your mother yet, but please do this. I will deal with her." And so they hadn't told me. Which is interesting because I feel that I am close to our girls, I would have said closer to them than William is. But they listened to him. Chrissy's husband, Michael, who is in finance, really listened, and he and Chrissy made arrangements to go to Connecticut to stay in the house of Michael's parents—his parents were in Florida, so Chrissy and Michael could stay in their house—but Becka balked, saying that her husband did not want to leave the city. Both girls said they wanted me to know what was going on, and their father said to them, "I'll take care of your mother, I promise, but get out of the city now."

A week later William called me and told me this, and I was not frightened but I was confused. "They're actually leaving?" I said, meaning Chrissy and Michael, and William said yes. "Everyone is going to be working from home soon," he said, and again I did not really understand it. He added, "Michael has asthma, so he should be especially careful."

I said, "He doesn't have terrible asthma, though," and William paused and then said, "Okay, Lucy."

Then he told me that his old friend Jerry had the virus and was on a ventilator. Jerry's wife also had the virus, but she was at home. "Oh Pill, I'm so sorry!" I said, yet I still did not get it, the importance of what was happening.

It's odd how the mind does not take in anything until it can.

The next day William called and said that Jerry had died. "Lucy, let me get you out of this city. You're not young, and you're scrawny and you never exercise. You're at risk. So let me pick you up and we'll go." He added, "Just for a few weeks."

"But what about Jerry's funeral?" I asked.

William said, "There will be no funeral, Lucy. We're in a—a mess."

"*Where* out of the city?" I asked.

"Out of the city," he said.

I told him I had appointments, I was supposed to see my accountant, and I was supposed to get my hair done. William said I should call my accountant and get an earlier appointment and to cancel my hair and to be ready to leave with him in two days.

I could not believe that Jerry had died. I mean that sincerely, I could not believe it. I had not seen Jerry in many years, and maybe that was why I was having trouble. But that Jerry had died: I could not get it into my head. He was one of the first people to die of the virus in New York City; I did not know that at the time.

But I got an earlier appointment with my accountant, and also for my hair, and when I went to my accountant's office I took the small elevator up: It always stops at every floor, he is on the fifteenth floor, and people squeeze in holding their paper coffee cups and then look down at their shoes until they get off, floor by floor. My accountant is a large, burly man, my age exactly, and we have always loved each other; it may sound a little strange, because we do not socialize, but he is one of my favorite people in a way, he has been so deeply kind to me over these many years. When I walked into his office he said "Safe distance," waving to me, and so I understood then that we would not hug as we always do. He joked about the virus, but I could tell he was nervous about it. When we were through with our meeting he said, "Why don't you go down the freight elevator, I can show you where it is. You'll be alone on it." I was surprised and I said, Oh no, there was no need for that. He waited a moment, and then he said, "Okay. Bye-bye, Lucy B," blowing me kisses, and I went down in the regular elevator to the street. "See you at the end of the year," I said to him; I remember saying that. And then I took the subway downtown to get my hair done.

I have never liked the woman who colors my hair—I had adored the first woman who colored it for years, but she moved to California—and the woman who took over, I just never liked her. And I did not like her that day. She was young and had a small child, and a new boyfriend, and I understood that day that she did not like her child, she was cold, and I thought: I am never coming back to you.

I do remember thinking that.

When I got home to my building I met a man in the elevator who said he had just gone to the gym on the second floor but the gym was closed. He seemed surprised about this. "Because of the virus," he said.

~

William called me that night and said, "Lucy, I'm picking you up tomorrow morning and we're leaving."

It was a strange thing; I mean that I was not alarmed but I was still kind of surprised at his insistence. "But where are we going?" I asked.

And he said, "The coast of Maine."

"*Maine?*" I said. "Are you *kidding*? We're going back to Maine?"

"I'll explain," he said. "Just please get yourself ready."

I called the girls to tell them what their father had suggested, and they both said "Just for a few weeks, Mom." Although Becka was not going anywhere. Her husband—his name is Trey, and he is a poet—wanted to stay in Brooklyn, and so she was going to stay with him.

iii

William showed up the next morning; he looked more like he had years ago, his hair was growing out and his mustache was coming back—it had been five months since he had shaved it off—but it was not nearly what it had once been, and he looked a little odd to me. I saw that on the back of his head was a bald spot; his scalp was pink. And, also, he seemed strange. He stood in my apartment with a look of anxiety as though I was not moving fast enough. He sat down on the couch and said, "Lucy, can we please go *now*?" So I tossed a few clothes into my little violet-colored suitcase and I left the dirty dishes from breakfast. The woman who helps clean my apartment, Marie, was coming the next day, and I don't like to leave dirty dishes for her, but William really wanted to get going. "Take your passport," he said. I turned and looked at him. "Why in the world would I take my passport?" I asked. And he shrugged and said, "Maybe we'll go to Canada." I went and got my passport, and then I picked up my laptop and put it back down. William said, "Take your computer, Lucy."

But I said, "No, I don't need it for only a couple of weeks. The iPad will be fine."

"I think you should take your computer," he said. But I did not.

William picked up the laptop and took it with him.

We went down in the elevator and I rolled my small suitcase to his car. I was wearing my new spring coat that I had recently bought. It was dark blue and black and the girls had convinced me to get it the last time we were at Bloomingdale's, a few weeks before.

iv

Here is what I did not know that morning in March: I did not know that I would never see my apartment again. I did not know that one of my friends and a family member would die of this virus. I did not know that my relationship with my daughters would change in ways I could never have anticipated. I did not know that my entire life would become something new.

These are the things I did not know that morning in March while I was walking to William's car with my little violet-colored rolling suitcase.

v

As we drove out of the city, I looked at the daffodils that were out by the side of my building and the trees blossoming near Gracie Mansion; the sun was streaming down with a gentle warmth, and people were walking along the sidewalk, and I thought: Oh, what a beautiful world, what a beautiful city! We got on the FDR, there was a lot of traffic as usual, and over to the left a group of men were playing basketball on a court surrounded by a chain link fence.

Once we were on the Cross Bronx Expressway, William

told me that he had rented a house in a town called Crosby—it was on the coast—and that Bob Burgess, Pam Carlson's ex-husband from years ago, lived there now and had found it for him. Pam Carlson is a woman that William had an affair with on and off for years, it doesn't matter. Anymore, I mean, it doesn't matter. But Pam is still friendly with William, and also with her ex-husband, Bob, and apparently Bob was a lawyer in that town and the woman who owned this house had recently put it on the market: Her husband had died, and she had gone into assisted living and she had asked Bob to manage the property. Bob said we could stay in the house; the rent was not even one quarter of the price of my apartment rent in New York, and William has money anyway.

"For how long?" I asked again.

He hesitated. "Maybe just a few weeks."

~

What is strange as I look back is how I simply did not know what was happening.

~

I had been kind of disheartened in the previous months. This is because my husband had died a year earlier; also I am often despondent at the end of a book tour, and this had been made worse because I no longer had David to call from the road. That was the hardest part of the tour for me: not having David to speak to each day.

Recently a writer I know—her name is Elsie Waters and her husband had died right before my husband David had died and so we were especially close because of that—had asked me to dinner and I had told her that I was too tired right then. That's okay, she had said, as soon as you are rested we will get together!

I always remember that as well.

~

At one point William stopped to get gas, and when I glanced into the backseat I saw what looked like surgical masks in a clear plastic bag and also a box of plastic gloves. I said, "What are those?"

"Don't worry about it," William said.

"But what *are* they?" I asked, and he said, "Don't worry about it, Lucy." But he put on a plastic glove to hold the gas nozzle, I did notice that. I thought he was really over-reacting to all of this, and I kind of rolled my eyes, but I did not say anything to him about it.

~

So William and I drove to Maine that day, it was a long sunny drive and I don't remember that we spoke that much. But William was upset that Becka was staying in the city, in Brooklyn. He said, "I told her I would pay for them to go to a house in Montauk, but they won't do it." He added, "Becka will be working from home soon, you'll see." Becka is a social worker for the city, and I said I didn't see how she could possibly work from home, and William just shook his head. Becka's husband, Trey, teaches poetry—he is an adjunct—at New York University, and I didn't see how he'd ever be able to work from home either. But I did not say that. In a way, I think it did not feel real; I mean because—oddly—I was not all that concerned.

vi

As we finally got off the highway in Maine and drove toward the town of Crosby, it was suddenly very overcast; I took my sunglasses off and everything looked really brown and bleak, and yet in a way that was interesting: There were many different shades of brown in the grasses that we passed by; there was a quietness to this. Then we drove into the town and there was a big white church at the top of a small hill, and there were brick sidewalks and white clapboard houses, and some brick houses too. You could see that the town was pretty in a certain way, if you care for such things.

I do not.

We stopped at Bob Burgess's home—a brick house in the center of town. The trees around it were gray and twiggy, without leaves, and the sky was grim too—and Bob came out and stood in the driveway a distance from the car. He was a big man with gray hair, and he wore a denim shirt and kind of droopy jeans, and he stood there leaning down to see us—William had the window open—and Bob said that the keys were on the front porch of the house, and he told us how to get there, and he said, "You will be quarantining yourselves for two weeks, right?" And William said Yes, we would. Bob said that he had put enough groceries in the house to last us that long. He seemed awfully nice as I tried to look past William to see him, but I did not fully understand why William did not get out of the car and why they did not shake hands, and as we drove away William said, "He's afraid of us. We just came from New York. In his mind we're toxic. And we could be."

~

We drove down a narrow road that went on and on; there were a few evergreen trees, but all the other trees were bare, and suddenly, as I gazed out the window of the car, I was amazed at what I saw. On both sides of the road was the ocean, but I had never seen an ocean like this one. Even with the overcast sky, it was unbelievably gorgeous to me; there were no beaches, just dark gray and brown rocks and spiky evergreen trees that seemed to grow right on the rocky ledges. A dark green water curled up over the rocks, and seaweed that was a brown-gold color, almost deep copper, lay wavy-like on the rocks as the dark green water splashed up. The rest of the ocean was dark gray and there were very small white waves farther from the coast, just a huge expanse of water and sky. We drove around a turn and right there was a little cove where many lobster boats were; and there seemed to be so much air, with these boats sitting in this little cove all pointing in the same direction and the open ocean behind them—and, honestly, I did think it was beautiful. I thought: This is the *sea*! It was like a foreign country to me. Except, in truth, foreign places always frighten me. I like places that are familiar.

~

The house we were to stay in looked large from the outside, and it was on the very end of a point, high up on a

cliff, with no other houses nearby; it was wooden, and
unpainted: weather-worn. A really steep, rocky driveway
took us up to the house; the car tilted side to side as we
drove up it. As soon as I stepped out I smelled the air, and
I understood that it was the ocean, the sea. But it was not
like Montauk, on the eastern point of Long Island, where
we had gone when the girls were small, or Grand Cayman; this was a bitingly salty smell, and I did not really
like it.

The house should have been lovely, I mean you could
see it had been lovely at one point, it had a huge glassed-in
porch that was right above the water; but as I walked inside I felt what I always feel about being in someone else's
house: I hated it. I hate the smell of other people's lives—
this smell was mixed in with the smell of the ocean—and
the glassed-in porch was actually thick plexiglass, and the
furniture was strange, except it wasn't—I mean it was tra-
ditional stuff, a sagging dark red couch and various chairs
and a wooden dining room table with lots of scratches on
it, and upstairs were three bedrooms with patchwork
quilts on each bed. Something about those quilts really
depressed me. And it was freezing cold. "William, I'm so
cold," I said, calling to him from the stairs, and he did not
look up at me but he went to the thermostat, and after a
few moments I could hear heat coming through the vents
on the floor by the side of the rooms. "Turn it up really

high," I said. The house was not as big as it looked from the outside with the huge porch, and it was fairly dark inside because of the porch. And because it was overcast. I walked around and put on almost every light in the house.

There was a slight dampness to everything. The kitchen and the living room looked out at the water, and as I stood there I thought again how astonishing it was, just open water; there were rocks, and the dark water was swirling over them in waves with a whiteness as they hit the rocks, it was something. Farther out I could see two islands, one was small and the other was bigger, and they had a few evergreen trees on them, and you could see the rocks that surrounded them.

There was a sweetness I felt at the sight of these two islands, and it reminded me of how when I was a child in our tiny house in the rural town of Amgash, Illinois, in the middle of fields of soybeans and corn there had been one tree in the field, and I had always thought of that tree as my friend. Now, as I looked at them, these two islands felt almost like that tree had once been to me then.

"Which bedroom do you want?" William asked me this as he put stuff from the car onto the living room floor.

The three bedrooms were not especially large, and the one in the far back had trees that came right up to the window, and I told William I did not want that bedroom but either one of the others, I didn't care. I watched him from the bottom of the stairs as he pulled my suitcase up, along with a canvas bag of his own stuff. "You get the skylight," he called out, and then I heard him go into one of the other bedrooms, and after a minute he appeared on the staircase with his winter coat, which he tossed down to me and said, "Put that on until you warm up." So I did, but I have always hated sitting inside a house with a coat on. I said, "I'm impressed that you knew enough to bring your winter coat. How did you know to bring this?" And he said, walking down the stairs, "Because it's Maine, which is northern, and it's March, and it's colder than New York." He did not say it meanly, I thought.

And so we settled in.

"We can't be with anyone for two weeks," William said.

"Not even to take a walk?" I asked.

"We can take a walk, but stay away from anyone."

"I won't *see* anyone," I said, and William, glancing through the window, said, "No, I suspect you won't."

I was not happy. I did not like the house and the cold, and I did not know how I felt about William. He seemed alarmist to me, and I do not like to be alarmed. We ate our first meal at the small round dining room table, pasta with tomato sauce. In the refrigerator were four bottles of white wine, and I was surprised when I saw them. "Bob got these for us?"

"For you," William said, and I said, "Did you tell him?" And he shrugged. "Maybe." William seldom drinks.

"Thank you," I said, and he raised his eyebrows at me then, and I felt a bit as I had on our trip to Grand Cayman that we had taken, months ago now, that William was a little odd to me, and he still did not have his full big mustache, and I could still not get used to it.

But I could do this for two weeks, I told myself.

Upstairs, I went into the back bedroom where the trees pressed up against the window and I saw then—I had not even noticed this before—that there was a big bookcase on the wall opposite the window with many books: mostly novels from the Victorian times, and history books especially about World War II. I took the quilt from that bed and put it over the one on the bed in my room. And when I fell asleep, I stayed asleep all night, which surprised me. It was a Thursday night, I remember that.

～

We got through the weekend, taking walks together and separately. It was so cloudy and there was no color any-

where except for the tiny patch of green lawn near the
house at the top of the cliff. I was restless. And I was cold
all the time. I cannot *stand* being cold. My childhood was
one of tremendous deprivation, and I was always cold
when I was young; I stayed after school each day just to be
warm. Even inside this house now, I wore two sweaters of
my own and William's cardigan over them.

vii

On that Monday morning, William was reading on his
computer and he said, "Did you know a writer named
Elsie Waters?" And I was surprised. "Yes," I said, and he
handed me his computer. This is how I found out that the
woman, Elsie Waters, the one I was supposed to have met
for dinner when I told her I was too tired—that she had
died of the virus.

"Oh my *God*!" I said. *"No!"*

Elsie was smiling brightly from the computer. "Take
this away," I said, handing the computer back to William.
Tears had come into my eyes, but they did not fall, and I
went and got my coat and took my phone and walked outside. *No, no, no,* I kept thinking; I was furious. And then
I called a friend of hers that I had known as well, and the
friend was crying. But I could not cry.

The friend told me that Elsie had died at home, that she had called 911 but when they got there she was no longer breathing. We spoke a few more minutes and I understood that I could not comfort this friend of ours, nor could she comfort me.

I walked and walked, as though in some tunnel; I kept wanting to cry, but I could not.

By the end of the week three other people I knew in New York had the virus; a few others had symptoms but could not get tested, because doctors did not want them in their offices. That scared me: that doctors were not letting people come to their offices!

I called Marie, who helped me clean my apartment, and I told her not to come to the apartment anymore; I did not want her on the subway. She said she had come the day after I left, but that she would not come again. Her husband was a doorman in my building, and she told me that he was driving in from Brooklyn—to avoid the subway—and that he would water my large plant every week. It is the only plant I have, I have had it for twenty years—I got it when I first moved out from William—and I am terribly attached to it. I thanked her profusely for this, for everything she had done. She sounded calm. She is religious, and she said she would pray for me.

~

I had already called the girls when we first arrived, but I called them again, and Chrissy sounded fine, but Becka seemed to be in a bad mood—querulous, I would say—and she didn't want to talk for long. "Sorry," she said to me, "I just kind of hate everything right now."

"That's understandable," I told her.

~

There was a big television stuck in the corner of the living room, and Bob Burgess had kept the cable hooked up. I very seldom watch television—we did not have one when I was a child, and I think partly that is the reason, I mean I never figured out a relationship to it—but William would turn this one on at night and so we watched the news. I didn't mind this, I felt it gave me (us) a connection to the world. There was news of the virus: Every day another state had more cases, but I still did not understand what was ahead. One night the Surgeon General said that things were apt to get worse before they got better. I do remember hearing that. And Broadway had already closed its theaters (!). I remember that as well.

~

What looked like an old toy chest was pushed up against the wall on the porch, and William and I found inside it an old game of Parcheesi. The corners of the box were so worn they were ripped, but William brought it out. And also we found a puzzle, it looked old but the pieces were there—for all we knew, the pieces were there—and it was a self-portrait of Van Gogh. I said, "I *hate* this kind of thing," and he said, "Lucy, we're in lockdown, stop hating everything." And he set it up on a small corner table in the living room. I helped him find the corners and the edges, and then I left it for the most part alone. I have never liked doing puzzles.

We played Parcheesi a few times, and I kept thinking: I can't wait for this to end. Meaning the game.

Meaning all of it.

viii

One week exactly after we got there, I called a doctor of mine in New York. He gives me my sleeping tablets and also pills for my panic attacks, and I called him because I was about to run out of these pills, and I had not slept well since I heard that Elsie Waters had died. The doctor was no longer in the city himself, he had gone to Connecticut, and he told me that day to wash my clothes after I had been to the supermarket. *"Seriously?"* I asked, and he said, "Yes." I told him that William was the one who would probably go to the grocery store when we got done quarantining, and he said, Well, then William should wash his clothes when he came home from shopping.

I couldn't believe that. "Seriously?" I asked again, and he said, Yes, it should be no different from washing your clothes after a workout.

I said, "But how long do you think this will last?" And he said, "We got onto it late, I'm guessing over a year."

A year.

This was the first time I felt a really—really—deep apprehension, and yet it was slow, that piece of knowledge, making its way into me, weirdly slow, and when I told William the doctor had said that, William didn't say anything, and I understood that William was not surprised. "Did you *know* that?" I asked him, and he only said, "Lucy, none of us knows anything." So what came to me then was the—slow, it seemed very slow—understanding that I was not going to see New York again for a really long time.

"And you should wash your clothes after you go grocery shopping," I said. William just nodded.

. . .

I felt terribly sad, like a child, and I thought of the children's book *Heidi* that I had read in my youth, and of how she had been sent somewhere and she was so sad that she walked in her sleep. For some reason this image of Heidi kept going through my mind. I would not be able to go home, and this sank into me deeper all the time.

~

And then:

On the television, William and I watched as New York suddenly exploded with a ghastliness that I seemed almost not able to take in. Every night William and I watched as New York City arrived to us in horrifying scenes, picture after picture of people being taken to emergency rooms, on ventilators, hospital workers without the right masks or gloves, and people kept dying and dying. Ambulances rushing down the streets. These were streets that I knew, this was my home!

I watched it, believing it, I mean I knew it was happening is what I mean, but to describe my mind as I watched this is difficult. It was as though there was a distance between the television and myself. And of course there was.

But my *mind* felt like it had stepped back and was watching it from a real distance, even as I felt the sense of horror. Even now, many months later, I have a memory of watching a pale yellow image on the television, it must have been the nurses in their garb, or maybe people wrapped in blankets on their way into the hospitals, but in my mind is this strange yellowish memory from watching the television on those nights. We (I) became addicted—it seemed to me—to watching the news on the television every night.

I worried about the ambulance workers, that they would all get sick, and the people working in the hospitals too. I thought of a blind man I sometimes helped off the bus near the bus stop by my apartment, and I was worried about him, would he now dare take anyone's arm? And the bus drivers too! All those people they came into contact with—!

And also I noticed something about myself as I watched the news during this time. Which is that my eyes would drop to the floor, I mean I could not look at it all the time. I thought: It is as though somebody is lying to me, and I cannot look at someone who is lying to me. I did not think the news was lying to me—as I said, I understood it was

all true; I only want to tell you that for a number of days—
and it turned into weeks—I looked at the floor frequently
as we watched the news at night.

It is interesting how people endure things.

~

We called Becka every day during this time, and she said,
Mom, it's awful, there are refrigerator trucks right outside our apartment building filled with people who have
died, they're right there when I go outside, and also I can
see them through the window. "Oh dear God," I said.
"Don't go outside!" And she said she didn't except when
they really needed something. When we hung up I walked
around and around the house. I did not know where to
put my mind.

~

There was a feeling of mutedness.

Like my ears were plugged up as though I was underwater.

~

William had been right. Becka was now working from home, and her husband, Trey, was teaching his classes online. Becka said, "I'm trying to work in our bedroom and Trey works in the living room, and he complains that he can still hear me. We can't go out— What are we supposed to do? God, he gets so irritated," she said.

In Connecticut, Chrissy and her husband, Michael, were also working from home. Michael's parents had said they would stay in Florida so the two of them could have the house. There was a small guesthouse on the property. "I'm glad we're not stuck together in that, at least we have this whole place," Chrissy said.

ix

After the two weeks of quarantine, Bob Burgess came over to check on us. Apparently he had texted William that he would stop by, but William had gone out to get his first five thousand steps anyway, so I was alone when Bob drove up the driveway. I went out and met him; he was standing on the small lawn area by the cliff, and he asked, Did I want to come out and sit with him? He had brought a fold-up lawn chair, and there were fold-up lawn chairs on the porch of the house we were in. So I put on my spring coat with William's big cardigan over it and went and got one of the lawn chairs to go out and sit with Bob. He was wearing a mask that looked homemade, cloth with flowers in it, and I said, "Hold on," and I went back inside and got a mask from William's room—I found them in the clear plastic bag—and then we sat far apart from each other on the lawn chairs, I mean farther than we would have if not for the pandemic.

"Weird time," Bob said, leaning forward with his elbows on his knees, and I said, "Yes, it is so weird."

And it was so cold up there on top of that cliff, the wind was whipping around, but Bob did not seem cold; I put William's sweater partly over my head.

Bob leaned back and looked around, and I understood that he was shy—this came to me then—so I said, "Bob, I can't believe how good you've been to us. God. Thank you. And thank you for the wine too."

He looked at me then, he had pale blue eyes, and there was, I saw, a kind of sweet sadness to him. He was a big man, though not fat, and he had a gentleness in his face that made him look younger than he probably was, though with the mask it was hard to tell. "No problem. Glad to help you out. You know, William's been a friend of Pam's for years, so I was glad to be able to help you folks." I felt a sense of almost guilt—this was the woman, Bob's ex-wife, who had been sleeping with William way back, but

Bob gave no indication that he knew of this or, if he did, that it was still a problem in any way. He said, "My wife, Margaret, would be here, but to be honest she has a little prejudice against New Yorkers." He said this without guile, and I liked him for it. I said, "You mean, just because we're from New York?" And he waved a hand and said, "Oh yeah, a lot of people up here feel that way, that New Yorkers think they're better than others," and I said, "I get it." Because I did.

He hesitated and then said, "But, Lucy, I just wanted to tell you your memoir really knocked me out."

"You *read* it?" I asked.

"Oh yeah." He nodded. "Knocked my socks off. Margaret read it and she liked it too. She thought it was about mother-daughter stuff, but I thought it was about being poor. I came from—" Bob hesitated, then said, "lesser means myself. Margaret didn't, by the way, and I think maybe if you didn't come from—well, from poverty— your mind just goes over it, and you think it's about mothers and daughters, which it *is,* but it's really, or it was to me, about trying to cross class lines in this country and—"

I stopped him. "You are exactly right," I said, leaning forward a little bit. "*Thank* you for getting what that book was really about."

.   .   .

I couldn't stop thinking about Bob Burgess. Oh, he had made me feel so much less lonely! He had been worried about Becka and the refrigerator trucks outside her apartment; he had once lived in Brooklyn for many years and he had been so concerned about her. He told me how he had never had kids; he didn't have a high enough sperm count; he just told me that like he was talking about the color of the sky, but then he said it was the only thing in his life that made him sad, that he had never had kids, and I said I understood.

And then we had spoken of New York City. "God, I miss it," Bob said with a real shake of his head, and I said, Oh, I do too! I told him how the flowering trees were out when we left, that the city had looked so beautiful in the sunshine. Bob looked around. "Awful up here in March," he said. "And April," he added. "Just awful."

Bob had grown up in Maine, in the town of Shirley Falls, less than an hour away, and when he came back to Maine after spending all those years in New York with his first wife, Pam, where he had been a public defender, he had lived again in Shirley Falls with his current wife, Margaret. They had come to Crosby only a few years ago. Then Bob told me about the Winterbournes, the old couple whose house we were in. He said that Greg Winterbourne had taught at the college in Shirley Falls for years, that he was really an asshole, and that his wife was okay, a little crisp but better than Greg. I told him how I had been asked to give a reading at that very college years earlier and not one person showed up. I said that I'd realized the chairman had never advertised the event.

Bob could not get over that. He said he didn't know who the chairman of the English Department had been, but he shook his head. "Man," he said. I felt I could have talked to Bob for hours, and I thought he felt that way too. I wished I had told him to please come back. When he left he said, "Call if you need anything," folding up his lawn chair and walking away with it. And I only thanked him. I did not say: Please come back—!

~

William spoke frequently to Estelle—the wife who had left him last year—and to their daughter, Bridget. He had asked them to leave the city at the same time he had asked our girls, and Estelle did that, she went to stay with her mother in Larchmont, right outside of New York City, and she was there now with Bridget and her—Estelle's— new boyfriend. I was struck by William's tone as he spoke to both Estelle and Bridget; he spoke to them with great affection, and sometimes I would hear him laughing with Estelle, and when he got off the phone he might say, "Boy, she's got herself a loser," meaning the new boyfriend, but William never said it meanly. One day he said, "I don't see how that can end well." I never asked him anything about the man; it did not seem my business to do so.

"But are they okay? Are they safe?" I asked, and he said, Yes, they were fine, they were all managing. Mostly I did not hear these talks because he would go out on the porch or talk to them during his walk; he often FaceTimed with them.

One day I said, "William, aren't you *mad* at Estelle?" It had been less than a year since she had walked out on him. William is a parasitologist, and she had left while he was delivering a paper at a parasitology conference in San Francisco. When William returned home he found a note from Estelle saying that she was gone. She had taken most of the rugs and some of the furniture too.

William looked at me with slight surprise. "Oh Lucy. She's Estelle. How long can you be mad at Estelle."

And I understood. Estelle was an actor by trade, though I had only seen her in one play. But I had met her many times over the years and she was a friendly person, and sort of plucky, this is how I perceived her.

I did not ask about Joanne, who had been William's second wife. I assumed that Joanne was the one mad at William, since he was the one who had left her. I did not care about Joanne; she and William had been having an affair while we were married, and she had been a friend of mine. Her name never came up.

But William would tell me when Bridget was having a hard time about something—and it was usually Estelle's boyfriend. "God, that poor kid," William would say and shake his head. "The guy has no idea at all how to talk to a young girl, he never had children and he's just a jerk."

I felt bad for Bridget, and yet sometimes—not often, and I am not proud to say this—I was slightly irritated that William spoke to her and about her so often; we would be eating and he would be texting with her, and sometimes this irritated me. One time I said, "Would she rather be with you during this time?" And he looked surprised, then said, "I don't know." He added, "Even if she *thinks* she does, she wouldn't want that, no. She's her mother's daughter, there is no doubt about that."

If I had known what was in store for Becka, I would not have felt any resentment at all for Bridget.

TWO

i

About my husband David: I thought—of course!—of him a great deal during this time. I thought how he had had a bad hip from a childhood accident, and so couldn't exercise much, and I thought, Oh God, he would probably have died with this virus! Also, he had been a cellist with the Philharmonic, and they were closed down now. All Lincoln Center was closed down. This baffled me, I could not grasp it; I mean it made David seem even more gone to me somehow. When I went for my walks, I would think: David! Where *are* you? And also, I could not listen to the classical music he had played. I had the station on my phone, and once when I turned it on during a walk to listen to through my earphones, the music seemed to absolutely assault me with a screeching kind of vengeance.

~

I called my older brother each week, as I had done for years, and I called my sister each week, as I had also done.

My brother, Pete, had never left our tiny childhood house in that small town in Illinois, and he had lived in it alone since our parents died; he said his life was not much different with the pandemic. He said, "I've been socially distancing for sixty-six years." But he was always kind to me—he is a sad and gentle soul—on the telephone, and he found it interesting that I was in Maine with William.

My sister, Vicky, worked at a nursing home one town away from where my brother lived. Vicky has five children and the youngest, born later in Vicky's life, is a daughter who worked at the same nursing home as Vicky. I should just say here that when I was seventeen years old I won a full scholarship to a college outside of Chicago, and going there changed my life utterly. Completely, it changed my life. No one in our family had ever gone past high school. And so when Vicky's youngest daughter, Lila, won a similar scholarship to the same school a few years ago, I had been terribly excited for her. But she had come home after a year.

I was worried about both of them working in a nursing home, and my sister said, "Well, I have to work, Lucy." She said this grimly, she has been grim for years, and I understand why. Her life has not been easy. I still sent her money every month and she never acknowledged it and I did not blame her. Her husband had lost his job a few years earlier. In truth, it made me very sad to think of her, and to think of Lila, who had won that scholarship to college exactly as I had. I had wished so much that Lila's life would become something new. But she had not been able to do it.

Who knows why people are different? We are born with a certain nature, I think. And then the world takes its swings at us.

ii

After a few weeks, William said to me one night, "Lucy, I'm going to take over the cooking. Please do not take any offense. It's just something I'd like to do."

"No offense taken," I assured him. I have never been interested in food.

In my marriage to David he did most of the cooking, always making sure there was something for me to eat on the nights he was at the Philharmonic. Remembering now David's poking his nose into the refrigerator and bringing out a covered dish, saying, "Here, Lucy, here is your dinner for tonight"—recalling this, as I sat watching William in the kitchen, made a shiver go through my soul. At times I would have to turn away for a few seconds and squeeze my eyes shut tightly.

Each night William made something different. He made pasta sauce and he made pork chops, he made meatloaf and he cooked salmon. But he also made a mess in the kitchen and it was my job to clean up, which I did. He wanted a lot of praise for every meal he made—I noticed that—and so I praised him to the skies. It felt to me like I praised him to the skies, but he always asked, even after I had praised him, "So you liked it, it was good?"

"It was more than good," I would say. "It was *wonderful*." And then I'd get up to clean the kitchen.

I understand that this may be hard to believe, but it is true: When I was a child there was no salt or pepper shaker on our table. We were very poor, as I have said, and I realize that many people who are poor still have salt and pepper shakers in their house. But we did not. Many nights for supper we had molasses on a piece of white bread. I mention this because it was not until I was in college that I understood that food could taste good. There were a group of us who sat at the same table in the dining hall for dinner, and one night I noticed that the fellow who sat across from me—his name was John—I noticed that John picked up the salt and pepper shakers and shook both of them over the piece of meat on his plate. And so I did the same.

And I could not believe it!

I could not believe the difference that salt and pepper made.

(But I still have never been interested in food.)

iii

One day a man came up on the porch with packages; they were for me and they were from L.L.Bean. William was out walking, and when I opened the packages I saw that there was a winter coat in just my size, it was blue and fit me perfectly, and also two sweaters for me. And a pair of sneakers that were my size as well! "William!" I called out to him as he came up the driveway. "Look what you ordered for me!"

"Wash your hands," he said. Because I had opened the packages. So I did. I washed my hands.

William put the packages back out on the porch. Then he came inside and washed his hands too.

~

Each morning William took a walk before I got up; he was an early riser, and he got in his first five thousand steps. Even when it was overcast, as it often was, the light would wake me from the skylight, and I mentioned that to him each morning. When he got back I would have the cereal bowls set out; we had Cheerios, and we sat at the table and had our breakfast, and I—in a strange way—liked this; it was maybe my favorite part of each day. It had always been my favorite time of the day with my husband David. But I liked it now because William was—sort of, mostly—familiar to me, and there was always a small, but for me very real, sense of hope that maybe today would bring something different, that the pandemic would pass and we could go home. After we finished breakfast we would move into the living room, where we looked out at the water. It was very cold outside, and the sun did not shine much at all; the ocean stayed gray. After finishing my coffee, I would put on my new winter coat and I would take my walk.

The only place we could walk to was back down the road that led to the point. I walked without seeing people, though I sensed a person sometimes at a window watching me. The road was very narrow. The trees were bare, and I thought again how in New York there were already flowering trees, and tulips in front of the buildings. It seemed strange to me that the world of New York would remain so beautiful as all those people were dying.

One day as I walked I remembered this: Near where one of my New York friends lives—in the Village—was an old woman that my friend and I sometimes saw when it was very warm outside. The old woman lived in a sixth-floor walkup, and she would bring a folding chair out to the sidewalk and sit on it there; she said her apartment was too hot to be in. We had chatted with her a few times; she often was holding a blue paper cup of coffee that the man at the deli would give to her. Where was she now? She could not come sit on the sidewalk in New York! And how did she get her groceries? Was she still alive?

I thought then that William had been right to bring me up here, where I could walk freely even if I didn't see many people. The question of why some people are luckier than others—I have no answer for this.

~

On this narrow road that I walked, with the cold air coming at me, and the trees all so bare, were small houses close to the road. Some looked like summer cottages, others looked as though people lived in them all year round. In the front yard of one place were yellow metal lobster traps stacked up and a board leaning against them that had red painted buoys draping over it. Another place had many, many old boats off to the side—it was like a garbage dump for old boats—and near it was a trailer where I saw a man once, I waved to him and he did not wave back; I felt very self-conscious, partly because of how often I was walking this road. I walked until I got to the small cove we had driven past the first day we came here that had thrilled me so quietly; it still gave me a quiet sense of awe, and I would sit on a bench there and look at all those boats, some with tall things that went upward toward the sky, but they were not masts, they were metal and must have had something to do with fishing; others were lobster boats, and there were buoys in the water. At times there would be seagulls screeching as they swooped down toward the docks. There were two old wooden docks, and according to what the tide was, either they showed their high skinny legs—which were tall wooden poles—or they looked as though they sat almost on the water. And then I would walk back again.

One morning an old man was sitting on the front steps of a small house; he was smoking a cigarette; the steps were not even, they leaned slightly to one side. And the house was white but had not been painted in some time. The man waved with his cigarette, a small wave. I stopped walking and I said, "Hello, how are you?" And the old man said, "Oh, I'm doin' okay. How you doin'?" And I said, "Oh, okay." He inhaled on his cigarette. He said, "You stayin' at the Winterbourne place?" And I said that was right. "What's your name?" I asked, and he said, "Tom, what's yours?" And I said "Lucy," and he smiled a big smile and he said, "Now, that's an awful pretty name, dear." Only he said it "de-ah." His teeth looked as though they were dentures that were too large for him. We waved again and I continued on.

A few cars went by, and the road was so narrow that they had to slow down for me even as I tried to stay way over on the side of the road.

~

As I came back up the steep driveway that day I saw a big piece of cardboard stuck to the back window of William's car and in big letters someone had written on it: GET OUT OF HERE NEW YORKERS! GO HOME!!

I was really frightened, and when William came out to see it he was not happy, but he just ripped it up and put it into the recycling bin.

Three

i

It has been said that the second year of widowhood is worse than the first—the idea being, I think, that the shock has worn off and now one has to simply live with the loss, and I had been finding that to be true, even before I came to Maine with William. But now there were times I felt that I was just learning of David's death again for the first time. And I would be privately staggered by grief. And to be in this place where David had never been (!)— I was really dislocated is what I mean.

I did not speak of this to William.

William likes to fix things, and this could not be fixed.

And I also understood: Grief is a private thing. God, is it a private thing.

～

William tried to work online with his lab, but his assistant was no longer able to come into the lab, and they had phone calls about some experiment they had been trying to do, and he kept telling her not to worry. Then he said to me one day, "Screw it. The experiment was a stupid one anyway. I'm going to retire soon."

"You're really going to retire?" I asked. And he shrugged and said, Yeah, pretty soon, but he didn't feel like talking about it; this is what he said.

But William was able to read. I was surprised at how quickly he read the books he had brought with him—novels, and also biographies of the presidents and other people in history—and also books he found in the bedroom upstairs. But I could not read. I could not concentrate.

Those first weeks I often took a nap in the afternoon and I was surprised when I woke up; I had no sense of falling asleep. And when I woke I did not know where I was.

William went out for his second walk in the afternoon, and when he came back I often went for my second walk. I would sometimes see the old man sitting on his front steps smoking, and he always said, "Hello, de-ah!" And I would wave and say, "Hello, Tom!" And then I walked back to the house, up the long driveway that was so rocky and where branches were like large spiders arched over it.

This is how we lived.

It was strange.

ii

What kept bothering me in particular was this:

When I pictured my apartment in New York it seemed unreal to me. In some odd—indefinable—way, I did not like it. I mean I did not like to think of my apartment there; it unsettled me. But there was a sense that I was split in half. Half of me was in Maine with William. And half of me was back in New York in my apartment. But I couldn't go back, and so that half of me was like a shadow—that's the only way I can put it. When I thought of David's cello leaning against the wall in our bedroom there, it hurt me—but more than that, I turned away from it, and this nagged at me more and more, this feeling. It made me very anxious, is what I am saying.

~

I spoke to my friends in New York on the phone. An older woman I knew had the virus, but she seemed okay; she had no sense of smell or taste and had a lot of body aches, but that was it. Another woman's father had died of it. A couple I knew both had it and seemed to be recovering. One woman I knew did not leave her apartment at all.

~

The sadness on my chest seemed to rise and fall according to— To what? I did not know.

And the weather remained cold, bleak.

About my work I thought: I will never write another word again.

~

There was an old washing machine and a dryer in a back room and we took turns doing the laundry, there was not much to do, but I noticed that William washed his jeans every two days. I could not remember if he had done that when we were married; I did not think he had.

Four

i

Poking around in a back closet one day I found an old tablecloth and brought it out. It was round and it had faded flowers on it, and around the bottom of it were faded pink pompoms. "Oh, this is perfect," I said, and I put it on the dining room table.

"Are you kidding?" William asked, and I said No, I was not.

ii

At times when I thought of my husband David, I noticed it made me angry to think of him. *You have no idea what we are going through!* I thought, angrily. I did not want to be angry with him, even though I know that is a normal part of grieving. But I did not want it. There was also this about David: He had not come to me in a dream and he had now been dead for almost a year and a half. When anyone else I knew had died, they always came to me in a dream, often more than one, and they arrived within a month or two of dying. It is always the same dream, they are in a hurry to get back to dead-land, but they want to know if I am all right, or sometimes they have a message for me to give to someone. This has happened to me so frequently that I stopped mentioning it to people— a friend of mine said once when I told her, "Oh, the mind does interesting things"—but I have always taken comfort in these dreams. Even my mother, in spite of how difficult she had been during my life, even she—years ago she had died—had come to me in a dream, twice she had come, and she was sort of anxious, as I said, to return to her place of being dead, but she had asked me if I was okay.

The same was true when Catherine—William's mother— died.

But David—he was gone. It was as though he had just disappeared down a dark hole, and now I thought: Jesus, David! Come *on*!

iii

One night as we watched the news from New York City we saw the trenches that had been dug on Hart Island—

this is in the western part of Long Island Sound, just off the Bronx—and we saw the many, many wooden boxes that were piled up in them: all the people from the city who had died of the virus and had no one to claim their bodies. I looked at the floor again, but I could not stop seeing the image in my head, the red clay dirt and the long pale wooden boxes one on top of another, unevenly placed in these deep, uneven graves. With the yellow excavators nearby.

Almost always, there was that sense of being underwater; of things not being real.

~

In the morning William said we needed more groceries and he would go to the store, did I want to come; he had gone a few times without me, and he had gone to the drugstore to get my pills. Each time he went to the grocery store he came home with stories of how depleted the shelves were: There was no toilet paper, or paper towels, or cleaning materials, or even chicken. This frightened me; I thought: We are in trouble! But William still carried on, and he had found two rolls of toilet paper in a small store on a back road.

That morning I said Yes, I wanted to go with him. And

he said, "Okay, but you stay in the car. No reason to put us both at risk." So we drove into town and parked in the parking lot of the grocery store, and William put on his mask and gloves and went inside. I did not mind staying in the car. And there were many people to watch! There was a faint reverberation in my heart as I watched them. Most of them were wearing handmade masks, and by that I mean the kind Bob Burgess wore, not the kind that William wore, which was paper and blue and looked surgical. But then I saw a mother speaking harshly to her son as they were loading their car, the kid must have been nine years old at the most, and that woman, I hated her; the son looked so unhappy; he had large dark eyes.

Everyone else was intriguing to me. Mostly women, but some men, and their lives were mysteries to me. They wore clothes I would not have worn; many women wore leggings—even in this cold!—going right to their waist, not being covered by any of the sweatshirts they had on. No one—that I could see—wore any makeup at all.

And then a woman started to yell. I wasn't sure what had happened, but she seemed to be looking at me, and she came closer to our car; she was middle-aged and skinny and her hair was half white but sort of orangey and she looked at me with fury. She wore no mask. I couldn't get the window down, because I would have had to start the car, and I was too mixed up by this woman who was yelling at me, and then I heard her say, "You goddamn New Yorkers! Get the hell out of our state!" She kept thrusting her arm out to the side. People were looking at her and she kept standing there yelling, and finally someone—a man—said, "Hey, leave her alone—"

And the woman went away, but I was so embarrassed because people were looking at me, and I looked down at my hands until William came out. He put the groceries in the back of the car; he did it as though he was irritated, and so it wasn't until we drove away that I told him what had happened, and he shook his head and said nothing. I said, "William, I *hated* getting yelled at!"

He said, not nicely, "Nobody likes getting yelled at, Lucy."

He said nothing else the whole ride home.

When we got back to the house William cut an orange into four pieces and ate them, and the sound he made, slurping them, made me go upstairs to the bedroom I was staying in. "They had toilet paper," he called out to me.

Mom, I cried inside myself to the nice mother I had made up, *Mom, I can't do this!* And the nice mother I had made up said, You are really doing so well, honey. *But, Mom, I hate this!* And she said, I know, honey. Just hang in there and it will end.

But it did not seem like it would end.

~

I should say this:

It was during this time that I noticed that I hated William each night after dinner. It was usually because I felt that he was not really listening to me. His eyes—when he glanced at me as I spoke—seemed to not really be looking at me, and it made me remember how much he could not listen. Or listen well. I would think: He is not David! And then I would think: He's not Bob Burgess! Sometimes I would have to leave the house in the dark and walk down by the water, swearing out loud.

~

The day after we had gone to the grocery store it rained, and by afternoon I was so restless that I took a walk with an old umbrella I had found on the porch. When I came back I said to William, as I sat down on the couch, "You weren't even nice to me after that woman yelled at me. Why couldn't you have been nice?"

The rain was hitting against the windows, and outside the ocean splashed on the rocks and all seemed brown and gray. William got up and went and stood in the doorway of the living room, and when he didn't say anything I looked up. "Lucy," he said. He said it with difficulty. "Lucy, yours is the life I wanted to save." He walked over toward me but he did not sit down. "My own life I care very little about these days, except I know the girls still depend on me, especially Bridget; she's still just a kid. But, Lucy, if *you* should die from this, it would—" He shook his head with weariness. "I only wanted to save your life, and so what if some woman yelled at you."

iv

One night after that rainy day I saw a sunset. It had been cloudy all day, and just before the sun went down the clouds had broken, and the clouds were suddenly a brilliant orange that spread up against the sky, I could not believe it, and the color got sent back over the water toward the house. You had to stand on our porch and look through the far window to see it, but the sky kept changing as the sun set farther, higher and higher the deep red went. I called to William and he came and we stood there for many minutes, and then we finally pulled up chairs to

watch it. What a *thing*! And so we watched for these sun-
sets as time went by, and sometimes they arrived: the most
golden orange glory in the world, it seemed to me at those
times.

~

Bob Burgess showed up with two Maine license plates,
and he said, "I'll put these on for you." He winked at me
above his mask, and we walked over to the car with him.
"Where'd you get those?" William asked, and Bob just
shrugged. "Consider me your lawyer. Let's just say you
don't need to know. There are always plates lying around
somewhere, and right now no one's going to notice that
these are out of date." He had on cloth workman's gloves
and he handed the New York plates to William after he
got them off. Then he stayed and visited—we all three sat
on lawn chairs on the little patch of grass on top of the
cliff, and Bob said that Margaret wanted to meet me,
would that be okay if she stopped by with him sometime,
and I said, Of course! But I wished that I could always see
Bob alone. When he left that day as William and I were
putting the lawn chairs back on our porch I said, "I love
that guy," and William said nothing.

~

The weather stayed awful almost all the time. Cold and brown and windy. But one day in the middle of April the sun came out and William and I walked out on the rocks—it was low tide—and then we walked to a closed store that was the only other building out on this point and it had a lawn near it, and there were rocks right there too, and we sat in the sun on the porch of this closed store. And we were happy.

That was the first time William noticed the guard tower. It was far off to the left, and he kept saying, "I wonder what that is?" And I looked and it was just a brown tower in the distance, and I did not care.

We sat for a long time in the sun; the water that stretched out endlessly before us had a large streak of white from the reflection of the sun. It sort of twinkled, but mostly it was just a bright, bright white that was on a huge strip of the sea. I got up to walk toward the water and I found a robin's egg, entirely whole except for the smallest crack in the bottom of it, so the yolk had caused it to be stuck to a small rock. Oh, it was a thing of beauty! "Look at this!" I yelled to William, and he pulled out his phone to take a picture of me, he was standing on the sloping jagged rocks, and he started to lose his balance; I watched it like slow motion and I watched as he staggered back and back and then to the side, and then he regained himself. "No big deal," he said, but I could see that he was shaken. "Oh William, you *scared* me," I said, and I ran to hug him. We went back to the house after that, but we were still happy and I put the robin's egg stuck to the rock on the mantel above the fireplace.

~

That night when I went into my room to sleep I found a sleep mask on the pillow. "William," I called out, "what is this?"

He yelled in from the room next to mine. "You're always complaining about the skylight. And the sun rises earlier these days. I picked that up for you at the drugstore that day and then I forgot about it—"

I went and stood in his doorway. "Well, thank you," I said. And he just waved a hand, his knees were up beneath the covers and he was reading. "Night, Lucy," he said.

~

I need to say: Even as all of this went on, even with the knowledge that my doctor had said it would be a year, I still did not . . . I don't know how to say it, but my mind was having trouble taking things in. It was as though each day was like a huge stretch of ice I had to walk over. And in the ice were small trees stuck there and twigs, this is the only way I can describe it, as though the world had become a different landscape and I had to make it through each day without knowing when it would stop, and it seemed it would not stop, and so I felt a great uneasiness. Often I woke in the night and would lie there perfectly still; I would take off my sleep mask and not move; it seemed hours I would lie there, but I do not know. As I lay there, different parts of my life would come to me.

I thought how when William and I first met—he was the teaching assistant in my biology class my sophomore year at college—I thought how, because of the tremendous isolation of my background, I had known nothing at all about popular culture, and I had known nothing, for instance, about the Marx Brothers, but when William would hold me, I would say, "Closer, closer," and he told me the Groucho Marx line where Groucho tells a woman who is saying that to him, "If I get any closer I'll be behind you."

Then the skylight would begin to lighten and I would put my sleep mask back on and fall back to sleep.

V

And then—oh God, poor Becka!

As I came through the door after my morning walk, this was toward the end of April, my telephone rang; it was Becka, and she was screaming, crying, "Mom! *Mom!* Oh Mommy!" She was crying so hard it was difficult for me to hear her, but the gist of it was this: Her husband, Trey, was having an affair, he had been planning on leaving Becka, he told her, but now they were stuck in lockdown. Becka had found texts on his phone.

I can almost not record this, it was so painful. Becka had gone up to the roof of their building in order to call me. In the background were the sounds of sirens, one after another.

"I'm going to give you to Dad," I said, and I did, and William spoke to her with precision. He asked her certain things: how long had it been going on, where had Trey thought he was going to live, was the other person married. He asked her things I never would have thought to ask her. And I could hear her voice getting calmer as she spoke to him. He asked her if she wanted to stay with Trey, and I could hear her say, "No."

"You're absolutely sure," William said, and I could hear Becka say, "I'm sure."

"All right, then," William said, "we're going to work on a way to get you out of New York. I don't know how, but we will. Hang in there, kid."

He handed the phone back to me, and Becka started to cry again. "Mom, I'm so humiliated, Mom, I didn't even know, Mom, I hate him so much, oh Mommy. . . ." And I listened and I said, I know, I know. I took the phone and went back outside with it, and I walked back and forth as my poor child sobbed.

When I came back inside the house William was on his phone; he was sitting at the dining room table. "Well, Trey," he said, looking up at me, raising his eyebrows, "what was your plan? How long were you thinking of continuing to deceive Becka?"

He put the phone on the table and put it on speaker and I could hear Trey, who sounded frightened, saying, "I don't have any answers for that, Will." After a moment Trey added, "I understand you're concerned for her, and so am I. But I think you should let us be the ones to work this out."

"Is that right," said William. "You think you should be left alone in an apartment with my daughter during a raging pandemic while you text love notes to some other woman?"

I heard my son-in-law's voice; he became angry, and he said to William, "You did the same thing to your wife, from what Becka has told me. I don't think you should be throwing stones in a glass house."

William looked at me, his eyes widening. He leaned over the phone; I could see him hesitate, I could see his rage rush up, and he said, "Yeah. I did, Trey. And you know *why* I did? Because *I* was an asshole! That's why *I* did it, you fucking numbnuts." He sat back, then sat forward again. "Welcome to the asshole club. *Asshole*." And our son-in-law hung up.

I remembered something then: When I had found out about William's affairs, I had gone onto the roof of our building too one day to cry; the girls must have been home, or maybe I didn't want the neighbors to hear me. But I went up on the roof and I cried and cried, and I remember saying out loud, "Mom, oh Mommy!" This was before I had made up the mother who is always nice to me, and so it was my real mother that I was calling out to that day. Crying for my mother—it was so primal, and that's what Becka's cries were to me.

That I could not be with her to hold her to me was anguish.

I felt almost out of my head with distress, is what I mean.

But William said, "She's going to be okay, you know." And that was hard for me, and I said, "Well, she isn't okay right now!" And he stood up and said, "Take the long view, Lucy. You never liked him. She's rid of him. She's a great kid, she really is. Now she can find someone else." He opened his hand and added, "Or not. Not everyone has to be married, you know." Then he said, "She married him on the rebound, don't forget." And of course this thought had gone through my head: Becka had been seeing a young man she loved deeply and he had broken up with her, and then she had very quickly met Trey. But I could not stop the feeling that I had been gutted. That Becka had been gutted.

William did not talk much during this time. But once he stopped as he walked across the living room and he said, "That fucking numbnuts is a *poet*? And all he could come up with is a cliché about throwing stones in glass houses? Jesus!"

I thought William made a good point. But I did not say so.

Two days went by. Becka phoned me a few times each day and wept and was angry—furious—and I could hear at one point Trey shouting to her sarcastically, "Mommy, Mommy, Mommy!" And I hated him then with all my heart. I could almost not stand it, I felt a violence toward him. I felt I could have hit him again and again if I was in his presence. It has always been frightening for me when I feel that rage toward someone. I had felt it toward a few of the women that William had had affairs with years ago. One woman, I had pictured hitting her face repeatedly. And it scared me, because of the violence I had had done to me by my mother when I was a child.

Chrissy's husband, Michael, called William and said he would be willing to drive into Brooklyn and get Becka; she could stay in the guesthouse on his parents' property for two weeks of self-quarantine, and when William told me that Michael had called and suggested that—let me only say that I loved him *fully*, I loved him as much as I hated Trey. It was unbelievable to me that he would offer this, I will never forget it.

But William said no.

William said that he was not going to endanger three people. I was aghast.

William looked at me and said indignantly, "You think I'm not getting her out of there? I'm getting her out the safest way possible, Lucy!" He added, "Michael has asthma, Lucy. Have you forgotten that?"

. . .

So William made a phone call to the driver he had used for years, the fellow who would take him to the airport and pick him up whenever William went anywhere, to a conference or wherever it was that William had gone in the past. "Horik?" he said, and he took the phone out onto the porch. As he returned, he was still talking into the phone and he said, "Lysol spray, all over the car. Every crack of that car. Okay, thank you."

And then he told me that Horik had had no business for a few weeks now, or very little business, and he said that he trusted the man completely, that he had told him his daughter's life depended on the car being clean. Then William called Becka and told her to be ready at nine the next morning. "The guy is not going to open the door for you, you just take one suitcase that you can lift and get in the backseat. He will text you as he pulls up to the curb." He added, "Wear a mask and gloves. Horik has to stay safe as well."

And so that is how Becka got to Connecticut and into the guesthouse. Horik dropped her off and Chrissy and Michael were waiting in the driveway, though they stood a long way from her, and Chrissy yelled to her, "The place is all made up for you!" Chrissy brought Becka's food to the door for two weeks, and Becka did not get the virus. They were—for me—a terrible two weeks and I spoke to Becka

each day, and yet toward the end of the two weeks I could
hear a change in her voice, she was more collected. She
always said, "Can you put Dad on?" And I did. I was
struck by this, and it made me feel more warmly toward
William, that his daughter wanted to speak to him as
much as she did to me, during this time of her enormous
distress.

When Becka's self-quarantine was up, she stayed in the
little guesthouse. "I like it here, Mom, it's so cozy," she
said. "And I can see Chrissy any time now, and we all eat
together every night." She was still able to work online as
a social worker for the city of New York.

So there was that. Becka had survived, was surviving.

I have come now to think of this as The First Rescue Story.

The Second Rescue Story arrived a month later.

Though in the end, neither rescue was successful.

But somehow this made me care a great deal about Bridget;
she suddenly seemed very vulnerable to me, and it had
something to do with Becka. Once I even called Estelle
myself to see how they were doing, and she said, "Oh
Lucy, it's so nice to hear your voice!" She said Bridget went
up and down, and I said, Yes, so did I.

Five

i

It snowed on the first day of May. It snowed two inches, coming down in thick flakes and curling into the outside windowpanes, and I could not believe it. "I hate snow," I said, and William said tiredly, "I know you do, Lucy."

William came back from his afternoon walk—his shoulders were sopping wet from the snow that had fallen on him from the trees, his sneakers were soaked—and as he sat on the couch, unpeeling his wet socks, showing his white old feet, he said, "I walked over to that tower." I did not know at first what he meant. But he told me that he had researched it, and it was a tower built during World War II to look for submarines, and there really had been German submarines that came up to this coastline. He said that just a little farther down the coast two German spies had gotten off a submarine and made their way all the way from Maine to New York City. It was huge national news and they were convicted of espionage and sentenced to death. But President Truman had commuted their sentences, and eventually they were freed. William said, "Nobody even remembers this now, but those towers are there because the threat was *real*." I did not know what to say.

I have written about this before, but I should just say that William's father had been a German soldier and he had been captured in a ditch in France. He was sent as a prisoner of war to work on a potato farm in Maine, and he had fallen in love with the potato farmer's wife—this was Catherine, William's mother. Catherine had left the potato farmer and run off with the POW from Germany, although that took a year or so because William's father had had to go back to Europe after the war and do reparations.

During that time Catherine, it turned out, had a baby girl with the potato farmer, and then she left them both, her baby daughter and her potato farmer husband, because William's father had come back to America, to Massachusetts. And William had not known about this other child—this half-sister called Lois Bubar—until long after his mother had died, he learned about it, as I said, last year.

William's father had died when William was fourteen;

Catherine never remarried, she had doted on William, who thought he was an only child.

ii

It was a few days after William had walked to the guard tower that I was looking at my email when I saw something forwarded to me by my publicist. Do you know this woman? my publicist had written.

It was an email from Lois Bubar, William's half-sister. She had sent it to my publicist asking that it be forwarded to me. In just a paragraph she said that she had been thinking of me during this pandemic, she hoped very much that I was all right in New York City and that William was all right too. She ended by saying, "It was so pleasant to have met you that day, and ever since I have felt very sorry that I did not agree to see William. If you speak to him, could you please tell him that, and tell him that I wish only good things for him. Please tell him I hope he is safe. Sincerely, Lois Bubar."

I did not especially care about Lois Bubar right then, I will admit that. It was Becka that I could not stop thinking about.

• • •

But when William came back from his walk, I showed him the email, and I was a little surprised by his response. He sat down and stared out the window at the ocean and did not say a word. "William?" I finally asked, and he turned to look at me; he looked slightly stupefied. "I'm going to write to her," he said, and I said, "Okay." He spent the afternoon writing drafts of an email to this woman; only when Becka called did he put his computer down.

You can imagine how taken up I was with everything that was going on with Becka, but as time went by Becka sounded fairly good each time I spoke to her, increasingly so. She told me she had not been happy for a long time, and I said, How long? And she said she couldn't even remember, but she said that she didn't like Trey, and I said, "Okay, honey." She said she had been on the phone to her therapist twice a week; William was paying for that, and Becka sometimes quoted the therapist; she had seen this woman, this therapist, before, and had now started back up with her. I suddenly remembered how when Becka had seen this woman years earlier—after her father and I had split up—Becka had said to me one day, "Lauren says that you let Dad manipulate you." I never understood that, but I had not said anything about it.

One of these days in Maine when I was talking on the phone to Becka she said, "Mom, Trey was jealous of you," and I said, What in the world do you mean? And she said, "Your career." Then Becka added, "You know, his poetry *sucks*." And I remembered how awkward I'd always felt when I had gone with William and Estelle and David to a few of Trey's poetry readings, because privately I thought his poetry was so bad, and so now I said, "Let him go, Becka. Good riddance." And Becka said, "He thought you were just an older white woman writing about older white women." And I have to tell you, that stung me a bit. And I said, "And he is a young white guy writing about— Oh, never mind." But it distressed me; I was embarrassed.

"He's just an asswipe," said William when I told him this. "She's had her life saved by this, I'm telling you."

And it seemed maybe she had. Chrissy and Michael were clearly being good to her. But as I spoke to her she seemed increasingly distant from me, and one night she said, "Mom, this whole thing is exactly what I needed."

iii

And then one morning when I went out for my walk I saw a bright yellow dandelion growing by the edge of the driveway near the bottom of the hill. I stared at it; I could not stop staring at it. I leaned over and touched the top of its soft head. I thought: Oh my God! After that I began to see more and more dandelions on my walks. Dandelions had grown along the edge of the long dirt road we had lived on when I was a child, and I had picked a small bouquet of them for my mother one day when I was really little, and she was furious because they had stained the top of a new dress she had just made for me. But they still—after all these years—made my heart open with wonder.

~

Bob Burgess showed up again, this time with his wife, Margaret, and she made me nervous at first, I think because she was nervous. It was still cold, but there was a slice of sun that fell across the grass our lawn chairs were on. Margaret and Bob, both wearing homemade masks, had come over right after lunch, and so William was there, and the four of us sat on the small lawn—I was freezing, even in my new winter coat—far away from each other in lawn chairs. Margaret was a shapeless woman—I mean she seemed to be shapeless in her coat—but she had amazing eyes, very lively behind her glasses, and even with her mask on you could see her energy streaming out at you. It was the beginning of May by now, but still so cold. She asked if I needed anything, and I said, No, thank you.

And then she suddenly said, "I'm intimidated to meet you."

I was so surprised. I said, "*Intimidated?* By me? Oh Margaret. I'm just . . . just me."

"Yes, I can see that now," she said, and that confused me. I wanted to be talking to Bob, as William was, I did not want to be stuck with Margaret. But she asked about my girls, her eyes were very sparkly as she asked about them, so I told her about Becka's husband and how Becka and Chrissy and Michael were all in Connecticut together, and she seemed to really listen, I could see her listening, and she responded exactly right somehow. I cannot remember what she said, but I remember thinking, Oh, she is right here with me.

She told me that she was a Unitarian minister, and I asked her what that was like, and she told me all the things she did, the Alcoholics Anonymous group that had to stop meeting on Tuesday nights, they Zoomed the meetings now, she was afraid it was not as effective, and she told me how she Zoomed her services. It was interesting to think of her life, although I could not get a real sense of it.

They stayed an hour and then stood up to go. Bob said, "Hey, Lucy, how'd you like our little snowstorm?" And I said I hadn't liked it at all. "Can't stand it," Bob said. "Just can't stand that stuff when it comes in May, for crying out loud."

Margaret said, "Bob has a tendency to be negative." But she said it cheerfully, touching him lightly on his shoulder. I said I probably had that tendency too.

~

That night I could not sleep. I did not take a sleeping tablet because it did not matter if I slept or not, and I was not especially uncomfortable as I lay awake, I was thinking about Becka, and also about Bob Burgess, and I heard William get up and I thought he would go downstairs to read as he did sometimes when he couldn't sleep, but instead he stopped at my door—our bedroom doors were always open—and he whispered, "Lucy? Are you awake?"

I sat up in the dark and said, Yeah, I am.

And William came into the room and sat on the edge of the bed; there was just a little moonlight and so I could not see his face clearly, but I understood immediately that he was distressed. "Lucy," he said. And then nothing more. So I finally said, "What is it, Pill?"

"Don't you want to know what I wrote back to Lois Bubar?"

I sat up straighter and I said, "Oh my God, I'm so sorry I never asked. I had forgotten about her because of everything with Becka. Oh, I'm so sorry! Tell me what you wrote."

So William went and got his computer and he sat back down on the edge of my bed. I cannot remember exactly what he read to me, but it was very well written and he'd concluded by saying he thought now that he had lived the life of a boy and not a real man, and he was very sorry that this was the case. I guess many of us have regrets, he wrote, but my regrets seem to grow as I get older. And he finished by saying that he was terribly sorry that his mother had never spoken to him about his having a sister; he said he found it almost unforgivable, and he was deeply sorry. And he wished her only the best as well.

He looked at me with embarrassed expectation on his face. "That's beautiful," I said, "that's a really nice email. Did she get back to you?"

And he said, "She did. Just tonight." He read again from his computer. Lois had been extremely polite in what she wrote to him, saying she understood it was not his fault in any way that their mother had behaved as she had. I have pity for her in my heart these days, Lois wrote. I understand that you find it unforgivable, but please know that I no longer feel that way. Your (our) mother knew I would be well taken care of, and I was. And then Lois had written: I hope you won't mind if I sign this with love. Love, Lois—your sister.

"Are you *kidding*?" I said. "William, that's lovely!" Then I said, "Write her back right away and say you're pleased she signed it with love, and then you sign it with love. Or whatever."

"Oh, I will. I will." He sat there in the semi-darkness looking down at his closed computer.

"What's the matter?" I asked.

I saw him look over at me in the semi-darkness and he said, "Oh, nothing. I just make myself sick, that's all."

I waited, watching him, but he said no more. And so I said, "Because of Pam Carlson and Bob Burgess? Did he ever know about you and Pam?"

And William said, "No, she never told him. She was getting around quite a bit—"

"So were you," I said, but I did not say it meanly. I did not feel any meanness as I said it.

"I know, I know." William ran his hand over his hair. "He's a nice guy, isn't he."

And I said, "I love him."

"I know. You told me that." Then William said, and I thought it was so odd, "I wish I had been more like him."

"You wish you had married Margaret and gotten stuck up here in Maine?"

And he said quietly, "No. But you know what I mean. I watch Becka go through this hell, and that's what I did with you."

I thought about this. I said, "She's doing a lot better than I was at that point." It seemed to be true. Then I added, "But I think she really maybe hasn't liked him for a long time." And I thought about that, and William evidently thought about it as well, because he said, "So you still liked me when you found out?"

"Oh God, yes. I loved you."

William sighed hugely. "Oh Button," he said.

"Pillie, we don't need to have this conversation anymore."

"Okay," he said. Then he said, "Hey, do you know who I was thinking of today, just out of the blue? The Turners, do you remember them?"

And I said, "Yes, you know I think I heard she had a breakdown—"

And we talked then. We talked for hours, William sat up next to me in my bed, and we talked about all the people we had known together, what had become of them. And then we both got tired.

"Go to sleep," I said, and William stood up and said, "Nice talk, Lucy."

"Great talk," I said, and I could sort of feel us both smiling as he went back to his room next door.

iv

I got to know the tides; I mean I got to understand when they went out and came back in, and they comforted me. I would watch the swirling water as the tide came in, lapping its white swirl again and again upon the darkened rocks below us, and also against those two islands in front of us, and I would watch on days when the ocean seemed almost—briefly—flat, and I would watch the tide go out, leaving the wet rocks and the coppery yellowish seaweed. When I looked straight ahead there was nothing on the horizon past those two small islands, that is how far out the ocean went. I noticed how the sky tended to match the ocean; if the sky was gray—as it frequently was—the ocean seemed gray too, but when the sky was a bright blue, the ocean seemed a blue color, or sometimes a deep green if there were clouds and sun. The ocean was a huge comfort to me somehow, and those two islands were always there.

The sadness that rose and fell in me was like the tides.

~

But Becka seemed to disappear from me. I even felt she was avoiding me; I would call her and she would not call back for a day or two. When she did speak to me her voice was rather flat. "Mom, I'm really okay, please don't worry so much about me," she said. It hurt my heart with a heaviness as though a damp and dirty dishcloth lay across it.

But of course she was grieving her marriage, no matter how unhappy she may have been in it—this thought finally arrived to me. And I thought, Lucy, you are so stupid not to have realized that.

~

And then Elsie Waters came to me in a dream. She was anxious, but very much herself. She had come to check on me, and when she saw I was okay, she nodded and turned around and went back through a door. I understood the door was death. But I had been so glad to see her!

When I told William about the dream he said nothing. It annoyed me that he had nothing to say.

~

Every night we watched the news on the television, and I read it on my computer during the day. This will end, I kept thinking. This will have to end. And every night it did not end, or indicate in any way that it would ever end.

I asked William to explain to me about the virus and why it had gone so out of control and why they couldn't stop it and why they couldn't come up with a vaccine right away, and he did explain it to me. He added that it seemed to him there had to be a genetic component to it, that a person's genes determined whether the virus could get access to them in a serious way or not. This might be why it was affecting people so differently.

I went through the days— I don't know how I went through them.

~

But I will say this:

There were times, as William would sit at the small

table in the corner of the living room and work on that puzzle of Van Gogh's self-portrait, when I would suddenly sit across from him—as I said, I hate doing puzzles—but I might find a piece of Van Gogh's cheekbone, let's say, and I would snap it into place in the unfinished puzzle, and William would nod, "Good job, Lucy," and I would think to myself: I am not unhappy.

V

One morning as I started out on my walk, Bob Burgess was just pulling into the driveway. He stuck his head out of his car window and said, "How's my negative friend?" And I said, Bob, come for my walk with me! And so he parked the car and he and I walked, and he walked more slowly than I did. He was not, as I said, a small man, and he walked with his hands in the pockets of his jeans; they were baggy, sad-looking jeans. There was blue sky, but clouds kept blocking out the sun, and then the sun would shine again, a bright yellow.

"Boy, I'm missing New York," Bob said to me that day, and I said, "Oh, me too!" He said this was the time of year he'd usually make his annual trip down to see his brother, Jim, who lived there, and he'd sometimes see Pam when he was there as well. He told me he had met Pam at the University of Maine in Orono; she'd come from a small town in Massachusetts. He turned his face toward me and said, with his eyes laughing, "It snowed on September twenty-ninth of our senior year, and I said, Pam, we're out of here. And so we left for New York right after graduation. Ah, Lucy," Bob said, shaking his head slowly, "we were just kids."

"I get it," I said. "I do."

And then Bob told me again how he had grown up poor. "Not as poor as you were, though." He told me that day about his father's death. Bob had been four years old, and he and his twin sister, Susan, and his older brother, Jim, had been in the car at the top of the driveway, and their father—while the car was warming up—went down to check the mailbox at the bottom of the driveway. The car rolled down and drove over their father, killing him. Bob said, "All my life I thought I had done it. I thought I was the one who fiddled with the gearshift. My mother thought so too, and she was super nice to me, I think, as a result of that. She even sent me to a shrink, and believe me, nobody went to shrinks back then, but the guy couldn't do anything for me, I wouldn't talk." And then Bob told me how it had only been fifteen years ago when his brother, Jim, said to him—Jim was older and said he remembered the accident more than Bob could—that he, Jim, had been the one playing with the gears, that Bob had actually been in the backseat with his twin sister, Susan, and all his life Jim had never confessed this. Bob shook his head. "It kind of fucked me up when he told me that."

I said, "*God*, I should think so!"

Oh, we had a wonderful time on that walk. I told him about David, and how he had played the cello for the Philharmonic, and how he had been kicked out of the Hasidic Jewish community when he was only nineteen, I told him all sorts of things, and he kept turning his head to listen to me, his eyes kind above his mask. When I said that some days I felt like a fresh widow, he stopped walking and touched my shoulder briefly and said, "Of course you do, Lucy. You *are* a fresh widow, my God. Lucy."

We began to walk again.

I said, "It makes it all the stranger somehow for me to be up here," and he said, nodding, "Tell me how exactly."

So I told him it was weird to be with William—except that it wasn't always weird, I said, which made it extra weird—and to be out of New York, and to not know when anything was going to change, and Bob glanced at me as he walked his slow walk and he said, "I hear what you're saying, Lucy."

We sat on the bench that looked out over the sweet cove, even though we were not quite six feet apart, but he sat on one end and I sat on the other, and the sun shone down with that yellow glory, and Bob said, "Do you mind if I have a cigarette?" He took one out of its package and pulled his mask down below his mouth. "I hope you don't mind." He added, "Margaret thinks I gave up years ago when I married her, but this pandemic—I don't know—I guess it's made me anxious, every so often I really want a cigarette."

I told him I didn't mind at all, that I liked the smell of smoke, which is true, I always have. And Bob sucked down that cigarette so fast, my heart unfolded toward him even more. Two seagulls flew down to the dock and then back up far into the sky.

As we sat there I thought about Bob's brother, Jim, and how famous he had become as a lawyer defending the soul singer Wally Packer, who had been accused of killing his girlfriend. It had been a huge national trial, and Jim had gotten Wally Packer acquitted. So I said, "Jim always knew that Wally Packer was innocent, right?"

And Bob looked at me then; without his mask I could see his full expression and there was a great tenderness to it. He raised his arm as though to touch my shoulder, but he did not touch it and he put his arm back down. Then he said, "Oh Lucy, sweet thing." And I felt embarrassed. "So he was guilty?" I said. "Did Jim know that when he was defending him?"

Bob inhaled deeply, looking at me with his kind eyes,

then exhaled the smoke from the corner of his mouth. "Lucy, I used to do defense work myself, and I suspect Jim did what all defense attorneys do. I suspect he never asked Wally if he was guilty or not."

"Okay," I said. Then I said, "Thank you for being nice about it. I'm stupid, Bob. I've always been stupid about the world."

And Bob said, "You're not stupid about the human heart, Lucy. And I don't think you're stupid about the world." He paused and then said, "But I know what you're saying. I have a bit of that myself."

As we walked back to the house, we saw Tom sitting on his steps. I waved both my arms. "Hello, Tom!" I said. And he said, "Hello, de-ah." Then he nodded at Bob and said, "Mr. Burgess."

"Hello, Tom," Bob said, and we continued down the road.

"You know him?" I asked, and Bob glanced at me sideways and said, "I do. I suspect he was the one who put that sign on your car saying 'Go Home New Yorkers.'"

"No, he didn't. He and I have always been friends." But then I remembered that the sign had been there the day I first spoke to him. "Really?" I asked Bob.

Bob didn't answer, he just kept walking.

"Well, who cares," I said. "Tom and I are friends now."

Bob's eyes smiled at me above his mask. "Okay, Lucy," he said.

We had gotten back to his car. "Let's do this again," Bob said.

~

So the next week Bob and I walked again. Then as spring was suddenly—so quickly!—arriving, Bob said that Margaret wanted to walk with William and me as well, so William and I drove to town and then followed in our car behind Bob and Margaret's car down to the river walk, where there would be more room for the four of us to spread out. "Just please don't leave me stuck with Margaret," I said to William as we drove there.

He glanced over at me. "I thought you liked her," he said.

"I *do* like her!" I said. "I just don't want to be *stuck* with her."

Margaret was a fast walker, and so was William, and so they walked ahead of us, but honestly, it was pleasant; that was a pleasant morning. The walk was a tarred path that went alongside the river, which sparkled in the sun that day; the leaves had finally started to come out and there was a sense of green and bright light; I thought the trees looked like young girls, tentative in their beauty. And there were dandelions here and there in the grassy areas.

Margaret stopped to talk to a number of people we passed, her eyes twinkling as she spoke, and I saw that she asked about them, about their mothers and children, and things like that. She was a minister, after all—and she did seem to be good at it. I saw that she was a really good person, is what I am saying.

vi

William kept walking to the guard tower; frequently he went in the afternoon. Every time he went he seemed glum when he came back. I noticed this, but I did not know what to say about it, and since he said nothing about it either, I did not ask.

I did not know how I felt about William. My feelings changed about him, they went up and down like the tides. But William was very often not *there* in a certain way, and it reminded me of when I was married to him, and how often I had felt that. Sometimes now when I wanted to talk—I have always liked to talk—he would roll his eyes and put his computer down and say, "What is it, Lucy?"

And I hated that. So I would say, "Nothing. Forget it." And he would roll his eyes again and say, "Oh come on, Lucy. There was something you wanted to say. So say it."

So I might tell him about how Tom was often sitting on his front steps smoking. "Have you seen him? Do you know who I'm talking about?" And William nodded. "I like him so much," I said. And then I would not be able to go on, because William was so clearly bored. Even when I said that Bob had suggested it was Tom who'd left the sign on our car, William simply shrugged.

At such times, I could not stand him.

But there were other times, often right before we went upstairs to our rooms, where he would soften and talk to me pleasantly. I told myself: His wife just left him last year, he has not seen any of his daughters for a few months, we are in the middle of a pandemic, he can no longer really work. Go easy on him, Lucy.

But then this!

One night as we sat in the living room together— William was typing on his computer—I said, "William, did you *always* wash your jeans so often?"

William stopped typing and looked straight ahead. Then he closed his computer rather hard, I thought, and looked out the window at the dark. He glanced at me and said, "I had my prostate out, Lucy. I had prostate cancer in late October. I found out a few weeks after you and I had gone to Grand Cayman. And I had it out."

I waited a moment, and then I said quietly, "You did?"

William sank farther down into his chair and started to jiggle his foot, which was crossed over his other leg, and he said, "I did. Yes, I did. And I went to the guy who was supposed to be the best, and he botched it, Lucy."

I said, "What do you mean, he botched it?"

William passed a hand down over his lower middle and said, "It doesn't work anymore. I'm through. No pill can help me. The dickwad surgeon said to me—I was still in the recovery room—he said, 'I had to cut the nerve.' And I knew." William added, "I sometimes still pee in my pants a little bit."

I sat watching him. Finally I said, "Do the girls know this?"

And he looked surprised and said, No, he had never told them.

"You had cancer and you didn't *tell* us?"

"Don't accuse me, Lucy."

"No, no," I said. "No, I'm not. But I'm so sorry, William! Oh my God, I am just so sorry! William, this is—"

And he put up a hand as though to stop me.

So I stopped.

·   ·   ·

But William stood up a little later and said, "Here's a good piece of news, though."

"What?" I asked.

He went to the refrigerator and took out an apple. "Bob Burgess got me in to see his doctor, and my PSA is fine. I found out last month. I was due to have it checked and I was getting worried, but turns out it's okay." He bit into the apple. "For now."

I could not sleep that night. I kept thinking of William and how he had had cancer and had his prostate out and how he had never told anyone. "No one?" I had asked him cautiously, and he said that Jerry had been there for him in the hospital, and after, when he returned home. I'd asked— tentatively—if Estelle knew, and he'd said, No, why would he tell her?

Oh William, I thought— Oh my God. William.

What a thing for him to go through—and to go through alone!

And that dear Bob Burgess had helped him out— Oh Bob, I thought. Oh William!

No wonder William didn't care about my dream of Elsie Waters. No wonder he could not listen to me often. What a thing he had been through! Swiping his hand down toward the lower middle of himself, "I'm through," he had said.

William *through*?

Oh William. Oh dear God. William.

vii

And then a little past the middle of May, this happened:
The Second Rescue Story.

William had just gotten off the phone with Bridget and we
were getting ready to eat supper when his phone rang; I
saw on the front of his phone that it said CHRISSY. I sat
at the table while they talked. William's face looked concerned. "So what time will they be in Connecticut?" He
listened, and then he said, "But tell Michael to tell them to
go to a hotel." Then he said, "Okay, I'll call him." He listened more, then said, "Right, and she lives where? That's
not far. She is? Okay, get me Melvin's phone number,
Chrissy. Bye."

William walked around and then he banged his hand
hard on the arm of the couch, and he said, "Goddamn
piece of crap." He sat down at the table and looked at me.
"Melvin and Barbara are on their way back from Florida
tomorrow. They told the kids today. Turns out it's too
hot down there for Melvin to play golf, so they're coming

home. He's been in restaurants and at the golf club, stupid Barbara has been playing bridge with her fucking bridge club— Jesus Christ, Lucy! They *know* Michael has asthma! Are they really that stupid?"

I said nothing. I didn't know what to say. Finally I asked, "Do they want the kids to leave?"

"Oh no! No, not at all! They'll just live there as one big happy family—until they all get sick with Covid."

"But won't they go to a hotel for two weeks to quarantine?"

"Apparently that's not their plan," William said.

After a few minutes Michael called to give William his father's cell number, and I heard Michael speaking quietly to William. "Not your fault," William said. "We'll talk soon."

But Melvin did not answer his cellphone. William left him a message saying something to the effect of "Melvin, you've been an excellent lawyer all your life. But I am a scientist and I am asking you to quarantine yourselves for two weeks before you see the kids. Your son has asthma and this is not a good thing to have at this point in time." He said, "Go to your mother-in-law's condo, Michael said it's empty. And please call me back."

I had somehow not thought of Barbara's mother, who was still alive, that she lived a few miles away from Melvin and

Barbara, she had lived alone with two healthcare workers who came in to attend to her; her condo was a one-bedroom and the healthcare workers slept on the couch, I remembered that. But William told me she had just gone into assisted living right before the pandemic and the condo was not yet on the market.

Melvin did not call back.

After supper we sat silently in the living room until eight o'clock, and then William stood up and said, "Okay, Lucy, we're driving to Connecticut tomorrow. These are our kids, Michael is our kid. You'll have to pee your brains out first, because you're not using any public bathroom on the way. We'll make sandwiches and take them, and we'll leave at five A.M. I suggest you take a sleeping pill, because I'll need you to help drive on the way back, and I would like half a pill myself."

I asked him if we should have Estelle drive and meet us there with Bridget, but he shook his head and put up a hand as though to stop me.

At five in the morning we took off. William had gotten up at four-thirty and gone outside, and by the light of the porch he put our New York license plates back on the car. We drove quietly for a long part of the way, and I actually fell asleep for a few minutes. When I woke up the sun was streaming through the trees. As we got farther south the trees were all a darker green than they were in Maine; it was a beautiful day. There was not much traffic. We stopped at a rest area, and we each ate one of the sandwiches I had made, and then William peed in the woods, and I did too.

As we finally got to Connecticut and pulled into the town—it is a small town in southern Connecticut—William tossed me a mask and said, "Put that on." So I did. In much of the town the houses were small, ordinary-looking, but the street where Melvin and Barbara lived was lined with huge trees, with all their leaves shining brightly in the sun. And right before we pulled into the driveway—the house was a large one, set back from the road, it had a Tudor look to it—William stopped the car and put on a mask as well. Then he called Chrissy. "We're here," he said when she answered, and I heard her yell, "Where? You're *here*? Wait, Dad, you're *here*?"

"Come on out," he said, "because we're not coming in."

And there was Chrissy, walking out the front door. She looked unbelievably beautiful to me, there was a glow to her face as she put on her mask, and Michael came behind her, waving his hand, and then dear Becka came out and she looked so different, I could hardly believe it was her.

Her hair had grown long, way over her shoulders, and it was slightly curly and she had lost a little bit of weight, and she looked older. "Becka!" I called, and she smiled and said, "Hi, Mom."

"Chrissy!" I said. Oh *God* how I wanted to hug them! "Dad says no hugging," I said.

"He's right," Chrissy said, but she blew me kisses. Becka and Michael both put on masks that they had been holding in their hands.

And we stood there, the five of us, and it was very strange.

Michael said that his father had called twenty minutes ago, they were on their way from the airport. "Okay," said William. He nodded and said, "I will do my best, Michael. I hope you will excuse me, but I am going to try my best."

"Good luck," said Michael; he said this with defeat. And William said, "I know."

I could not stop looking at the girls; they were so grown-up-appearing, and they seemed a little awkward, as though they did not know what to do with us. So I said, "Let's sit by the pool," and so we all went over to the pool, which still had its cover on from way back before Michael's parents had gone to Florida before the pandemic. It was like a trampoline—the cover, I mean—only stuck into the ground with thick peg-like things. But there were plastic chairs around it and we arranged the chairs far apart and we sat down. Becka had a seriousness to her eyes, oh God, she broke my heart, but she seemed okay. Or perhaps she was pretending to be okay, I don't know, but Becka has never been able to pretend, is what I mean. I desperately wanted to speak to each child alone. "Becka," I said, "tell me how you are."

"I'm okay," she said, and I thought, Oh my God, she is lying, but she looked at me then and I saw—I thought I saw—a new maturity in her face, although with the mask on it was hard to know. "Please don't worry about me, Mom," she said. "I'm really okay." And then her eyes got very bright as she started to tell me about her work; she said how there was so much to do, because with all the schools closed there had been a rise in domestic abuse, but it wasn't getting reported enough, and she told me what she did on the computer about these things, and I was very interested and yet I could not quite listen, I could only watch her eyes, and how she flicked her hair back over her shoulder in a way that was new to me. And yet she was Becka through and through.

And then Chrissy, who is a lawyer for the American Civil Liberties Union, said she had tons and tons of work to do because with all the lockdowns they had to be careful about people's civil rights, and I noticed that William did not say anything to her as she spoke about this. But then he said, "Good for you, Chrissy."

A breeze made a green leaf scuttle across the pool's covering.

And then I asked Michael how his work was—he is an investor—and he said, "Man, it is just absolutely fucking crazy out there right now." And I said I understood.

Just as I was saying that, a black car pulled into the driveway and we all stood up hurriedly and walked toward the long circular driveway, and after a moment Melvin got out of the backseat; he was wearing kelly green slacks and a pink polo shirt, and then Barbara got out, she looked skinnier than ever, wearing a canvas hat, and Melvin took off his sunglasses and squinted in our direction and said, "What the—" Then he broke into a smile and said, "Hey— you two!" He stuck his hand out to shake William's hand.

I have always liked Melvin. He has a charm to him, he is youthful-looking, and I always sort of felt bad that he was married to Barbara, who I thought was never—since I had known her—a happy woman.

William said, "Hello, Melvin. Let's not shake hands, there's a pandemic going on."

"Look at you guys," and Melvin laughed. Without his sunglasses on you could see the whiteness of the laugh lines by his eyes; his face was that tanned. "You all look ready to do surgery. Holy Christ."

William said to Melvin, "Let's talk," and he indicated with his hand that the two of them should go back to the pool area.

"Okay then," said Melvin, with a small shake of his head. "But my God you're making me feel strange." He put his sunglasses back on.

The driver took suitcases and golf bags out of the trunk and leaned them against the car.

William stood while Melvin sat in a pool chair. I asked Barbara how she was, and she said, Oh, you know, she was fine, but she put her attention to Michael and asked after him and they talked about Michael's brother, who lived in Massachusetts, and I looked back at the girls, and they seemed tense, as was I, but we kept glancing at one another in a conspiratorial way and trying to chat.

Melvin finally pushed his chair back, noisily, and he stood up and he said, "Okay, okay."

I thought he'd be irritated but he came back smiling. He said, "Lucy, how are you?" And I said I was all right. Then he said to Michael, "Son, why don't you go inside and get the key for the SUV, I'd appreciate it. And then we'll leave you alone so you won't get our Florida *coo-*

ties." He turned and beamed at all of us, spreading his hands out, up and flat into the air with his fingers wiggling.

Michael went inside and came out and tossed a key to his father. His father caught it, and I was glad he did, I could tell it made him feel manly. Michael went to the garage and pushed a button and the door rose in front of the big black SUV. Melvin backed it out, and he put the suitcases in it, and the two bags of golf clubs, and then he said to his wife, "Let's go," and Barbara said, "Goodbye, Lucy."

"See you kids in two weeks," Melvin said, and they drove down the driveway.

We stood there, the five of us, all of us were serious. The breeze was picking up and you could hear the leaves of the trees rustling. I thought that William looked exhausted; his face was pale. Finally Chrissy said, "Thanks, Dad. Boy, thank you so much." And then Michael said the same. Becka was silent, she looked frightened. So we only stayed about twenty more minutes; my head felt very swimmy. William clapped his hands as though to try and be jovial and he said, "You kids are all doing just great. You all look wonderful." And they did. We spoke a little more, I don't remember about what.

But Becka walked me away for a moment, and she put

her hand up to block the sun from her eyes and said, "Mom, you know how we used to meet up at Bloomingdale's? Well, Chrissy and I were talking about Bloomingdale's the other day. It might have to close down, we don't know yet, but so many places are going out of business. But we were saying it doesn't matter if Bloomingdale's folds, because it's really a place of bad things when you actually think about it. I mean—Mom!—all that stuff made overseas by kids working for terrible wages, and it's just so materialistic, I can't believe I never thought about that, Mom. But it's gross. So when you come back to the city we're going to find a different place where we will meet you."

"Okay," I said. "That sounds wonderful. I'm very proud of you two. I look forward to it."

But I was surprised; I really was.

And then we walked back and we stood there with the others, and Becka said, "We can't even do a family hug." She started to cry then, and I said, "That's okay, we all got to see each other—" And Becka's sobs became deep, and I could barely stand them, my pain for her was so great. I looked at Chrissy and I remember thinking: Oh, she is like William, but I did not mean this in a bad way, I just meant that she was controlled.

"Becka," said William, "you have a family that loves you very much. Now we have to get going, we've had a long day, and we've got a long trip back." He raised his hand. "You all stay safe."

And Becka stopped her crying.

~

As soon as we were in the car William said not to talk to him, he was too tired. And then as we left Connecticut, William said, "Lucy, you have to drive, I'm dead." So we stopped and each ate another sandwich and then I drove. William fell asleep, his head dropped to his chest. I was worried about him, but as we got to the New Hampshire border he seemed to rouse himself, and he said, "The girls looked great."

"They looked wonderful," I said. Then I said, "William, what did you say to Melvin?"

William looked out the window on his side and then back at the windshield in front of him and he said, "Oh, I gave him time to tell me how stupid I was being—he said it jokingly, of course, being Melvin—and then I told him every single fact of the pandemic that he obviously did not know. And before he could suggest that *they* go to Barbara's mother's place, I told him there were three kids and two of them and only one bedroom there.

"And then," William looked over at me with a half-smile, "I told him that I knew a *New York Times* reporter who would love the story of a man coming back from Florida—a well-known lawyer, prominent—and infecting his asthmatic son because he just didn't believe that he could. The *Times* would eat that right up. Make a great story right now. That's what I told him."

"Well," I said, "it worked." After a minute I asked him, "Do you know someone at *The New York Times*?"

"Of course not," William said.

We drove into New Hampshire, and I said, "*Oh!* Chrissy's pregnant."

"Are you serious?" William looked at me. "She told you that and you're only now telling me?"

"No, she didn't tell me. I just now realized it."

William said, "You mean you had a vision?"

And I thought about it, and I said, "No, it wasn't a vision. But I think she's pregnant, William, and that was one reason she looked different."

"Why didn't you ask her?"

I glanced over at him. "She would have told me if she wanted me to know. And she's already had that one miscarriage, she may not want anyone to know until she's more along."

"I hope you're right," William said. Then he added, "But bringing a kid into this world, Jesus."

We drove farther, we were in Maine now. And then I did

have a vision; it had actually come to me the moment I saw Melvin step out of the car, it was as though he had—very briefly—an aura around him that was dark, and I have not had visions for a while, but that aura thing had come to me when I saw him, and it came again as we drove along, but now it was like a dark bird that flew across the windshield, so fast it was almost gone.

"Melvin's got the virus," I said.

~

That night there was a thunderstorm. It started just as we finally got back to Crosby, and it was magnificent. It was glorious to sit in that house and hear the rain coming down on the roof, and to see outside the lightning that lit up the ocean. The crack of thunder that came after each bolt of lightning across the water, it was just gorgeous, is all I want to say. We sat on the couch, holding hands—loosely—and for some reason the thunderstorm made me feel better. It might have made William feel better too, I am not sure, he sat and seemed far away. But he was exhausted. And so was I. I told him what Becka had said about Bloomingdale's and the materialism of it and how the things in it were made overseas at cheap prices. "It surprised me," I said.

He answered, "Ah, she's just saying that because she's young."

"She's not that young," I said, and he said that he knew that.

Then he said, squinting toward the window, "But what she says is true."

~

Four days after we got home, Melvin went into the hospital; he had the virus, and he stayed in the hospital for ten days. Barbara also had the virus, but she did not have to go to the hospital. Barbara's mother got the virus as well in the assisted-living place she lived in, but it did not kill her. Melvin and Barbara went on living in her mother's condo, and the same women who'd come to help Barbara's mother came to help them. "Oh my *God*!" I said when Chrissy called to tell us, and I asked that she put Michael on, and he was subdued but he said, "It was good of William to have kept them out of the house, Lucy," and I thought that was decent of him, because his father had just been very sick.

I kept walking around the house thinking, Melvin almost died! I could not believe it, although I knew it was true.

viii

On the news one night was a segment about Bangladesh and the shops where clothes were made, and it showed how the workers were not even given masks and also many of them had lost their jobs because no one was buying clothes right now, but the images of these very young girls, crowded into huge rooms, trying to cut pieces of fabric as quickly as they could—

It made me understand that Bloomingdale's was exactly what Becka had said it was, a place where many bad things were manifested, and there we had been, the three of us so innocently, so stupidly, enjoying it, as though we could do that forever. Sauntering through the shoe section like that was all we had to do in the world.

~

That night I could not fall asleep, and my mind went to different places as it did on such nights, and I remembered this:

Years ago in New York City I had taught at a community college and there was a man who taught there as well, he was much older than I was, and he retired soon after I got there. He was a nice man, with thick eyebrows, and he was quiet, though he seemed to like me and we would sometimes talk in the hallways. He told me that his wife had Alzheimer's, and that he could not remember the last word she had spoken to him, because she'd become gradually more and more silent and then she remained silent. And this man, her husband, could never remember the last thing she had said.

And thinking of this now made me think of something I had often thought before: that there had been a last time—when they were little—that I had picked up the girls. This had often broken my heart, to realize that you never know the last time you pick up a child. Maybe you say "Oh, honey, you're getting too big to be picked up" or something like that. But then you never pick them up again.

And living with this pandemic was like that. You did not know.

BOOK TWO

One

i

Toward the end of July, I had a massive panic attack, and as a result, many things in my life changed; huge changes were made.

But let me mention some sad things that happened before that event, even some terrible things, and some good—even lovely—things that happened as well.

~

The first terrible thing that happened was this:

At the end of May a policeman knelt for nine minutes and twenty-nine seconds on the side of a Black man's neck. The man's name was George Floyd. You could watch this on video as George Floyd said, "I can't breathe, I cannot breathe," and the policeman had no expression on his face as he knelt on the neck of that man, George Floyd, who died.

This happened in Minneapolis, and the protests started there and then moved throughout many different cities in the country, even around the world; night after night we watched on the television as people protested, and at times there were flames that reached into the night sky, and storefronts were smashed while great crowds of people protested the murder of yet another innocent Black man, George Floyd.

I thought, "Oh God, they will all get sick." But I felt more than that. I understood the anger, I *really* did.

Night after night we watched the television: Portland, Oregon, was especially having trouble. The protesters were being threatened by others, and also the police were involved. It terrified me. In New York, people took to the streets again and again.

As all this happened I felt both hopeless and also hopeful. It was as though the racism in this country had suddenly exploded, hurling forth. But people were *caring* about this! Many were.

I remembered this: Years earlier, when William and I were still married, a young Black man—his name was Abner

Louima, I looked it up online to remind myself after the death of George Floyd—had been arrested in New York, and one of the policemen who arrested him sodomized him with a broom handle in the police station. I had had a deep response to this; I can still see the young man's face, I mean Abner Louima, who this happened to. He had given an interview from a hospital bed, and his face was an open face, a lovely face. And the policeman who had done this to him lived alone with his mother on Staten Island. And I hated that man; I hated the look on his face, with no remorse at all, his face stayed blank. And I remembered having that feeling of wanting to hit his face, which, as I have said, scares me. That feeling, I mean.

I have never hit another human being.

But I have had those feelings; they are hidden very deep inside me.

~

And then Becka texted me one day and said: Don't tell Dad but we've been going to the protests in New Haven. Don't worry, we are safe!

I called her immediately but she did not pick up.

I did not tell William. I thought how he had gone down there to Connecticut, trying to save their lives, and that he would worry—as I did—that they were now in crowds with no safe distancing. God, I worried. But I was really proud of them too.

There was for me during this time a sense of being dazed. As though, in a way, I was not capable of taking in everything that was happening in this world.

ii

The second thing that happened—which was a lovely thing—was this:

We started to make friends in Maine. We did this through Margaret and Bob; it was really summertime now, and they began to invite us to different places with different people—always safe-distancing outdoors and with masks—and I began to realize that I liked the people we met through them. They were varied.

I will get to them soon.

~

But I need to confess this first:

I went to the grocery store by myself one day; I went to get detergent and a few power bars, and more wine. There was a long line outside. People stood wearing masks, six feet apart—the store had laid down taped markers on the ground to indicate where we should stand—and waited to be summoned into the store. It was midafternoon on a cloudy Sunday, and as I parked the car I saw many people hurrying across the parking lot, and I understood—or felt that I did—that people wanted to get into the line quickly, because the line was growing longer by the second, it went around the building. I took my place in line behind a young man who kept looking at his phone, and as we got closer to the entrance of the store I saw a man—he was elderly and pale and had a look of being unwell—I watched him walking slowly across the parking lot, and I thought: Well, they will let him get in ahead of the line. But the man walked past me and I saw him getting toward the end of this long line. I thought: I should go and get him and let him trade places with me—because at that point I was only a few minutes from getting into the store.

I even looked around to see how long the line was, and it had gotten very long. I did not go and get the elderly man.

I did not do that.

A woman two places ahead of me—she looked my age, maybe just a few years younger—said to the young man behind her, the young man with the phone, "Hold my place in line." The young man did not look up from his phone, and I saw this woman go and get the elderly man from where he was walking, about to turn the corner of the building for the back of the line, and she walked him up to her place in the line, and he was able to get into the store right away, and then the woman who had done this looked around a bit, as though—maybe—wondering if she could get her own space back, but no one said anything, or even seemed to notice her, including the young man who was supposed to be saving her place, he was still looking at his phone, and I watched as she went around the building—I presume to the very back of the line; she had given up her spot and had to wait again.

And I thought: That should have been me. I should have done that for the elderly man.

But I had not done it.

I had not wanted to wait in the very long line, as this woman was now doing.

And I learned something that day.

About myself and people, and their self-interest.

I will never forget that I did not do that for that man.

iii

Before I tell you about the friends we were making, let me say that it was one afternoon in the first week of June that

William came back from his walk and said that the next day he was going to drive to Massachusetts and that Estelle would meet him at Old Sturbridge Village—there was a park there—with Bridget. "It's been far too long," he said, and he had a dark look as he said that.

I asked if he wanted me to go with him to help him with the drive, but he said No, it was only three hours each way, he could do that. I asked if Estelle was driving up by herself, and he said Yes, so I figured that she would not be bringing her loser boyfriend.

The next day William took off early in the morning. I had made him a tuna fish sandwich and he almost forgot it. "William," I called, following him out the door with the sandwich and a bottle of water, "take these!" And he took them from me. "Call me if you need me," I said, but he only waved his hand and got into the car—he had put the New York license plates back on again—and drove down the steep, rocky driveway.

It was funny. At first I was kind of glad to have him gone. There was a freedom to the house without him, I thought. I called a friend in New York and we spoke for a long time, and we laughed, and then I hung up and the house was silent. I went for a walk down by the water because it was low tide, and I loved seeing the different periwinkles, there were larger white ones and then many more smaller brown

ones. And sometimes—not often, and not that day—
a starfish. And always the seaweed, slippery and deep yel-
lowy brown, straggled across the rocks. So I did that, and
then I felt a little frightened, because I started to think my
balance was not all that good anymore, and what if I fell?
So that took the pleasure out of what I was doing, and
also the clouds were coming in—all day it had been a
beautiful shining day—and I went back up to the house,
and I thought: I will read. But there was nothing I wanted
to read. I could not read; as I said, I had been able to read
only very little since I'd arrived. And I could not write either.

It was not yet noontime.

I thought then of all the people who were enduring these
times alone. My friend in New York that I had just spoken
to was alone. Twice a week, behind her building, she sat at
one end of a table with a friend who sat at the other, far
end of this table, and they visited. With William away, I
thought of this differently now; I understood my friend's
predicament more, I mean. But my friend could read, and
I could not. Still, she was alone.

I wished I could see Bob Burgess. I wished the girls would
call me, but they did not, and I did not call them.

· · ·

So I lay down on the couch and I took my iPhone and my earbuds and started to listen to some classical music. This time I did not react the way I had the few other times when I had listened to the music that David (sometimes) used to play. This was the first time I was able to feel that I was lying on a soft cloud of an almost golden color, and I did not move because I was afraid the feeling would go away. I thought: I am resting! I was able to rest, and it was extraordinary.

At eight o'clock, as the sun was going down, William returned. I went to the door, but he did not come in, and so I stood there. After a moment I walked outside, and his car window must have been open, because then I heard him: He was weeping. He was sobbing. I went hurriedly out to the car, and his head was leaning on the steering wheel. He looked up at me, and he could not speak; water was all over his face. And he continued to weep like that.

"Oh Pillie," I whispered.

After another few moments he got out, and he let me hug him, but he did not hug me back. He followed me into the house and sat down on the couch, and I said, "What happened?"

And he said, "Nothing happened. It was fine. I'm just so sad, Lucy. I'm so sad."

I had only seen William weep like this one time before in our lives, and it was the day he told me about his affair with Joanne. She had been a friend of both of ours from college, and he had told me three months earlier about having different affairs, but when he told me about his affair with Joanne he wept as he was weeping now. He said that day, "I'm sick, Lucy. I'm a loser." I had never heard him say such a thing, and after a while he stopped crying. I did not cry about Joanne. I was too stricken, I was far too sad to cry. Joanne became his second wife, for seven years.

And now I could only watch him and wait, and he stopped his crying and said again, "It was fine, it was good to see them both." Apparently it was not until he had said good-bye to Bridget—she had started to cry—and watched Estelle drive away with his daughter in the passenger seat that he began, as he also drove away, to cry himself.

"Was Estelle nice to you?" I asked tentatively.

And William said, "Oh yeah. Of course. She was great, couldn't have been nicer." He shook his head and said with more strength, "It's just that I'm sad, Lucy."

And I understood.

Two

i

Here is one story about people we met through Margaret and Bob:

It was not quite the middle of June and the weather was really lovely, and Bob and Margaret invited us with another couple and we sat down at the marina—we took up two picnic tables a few feet away from each other, it was a beautiful evening, hardly a breeze even by the water, and the man of the other couple had just retired from working for the state in the Department of Health and Human Services, and his wife was a social worker at the hospital in town.

The wife's name was Katherine Caskey, and she sat at the far end of the table across from me, and Bob sat across from me at the other far end of the table. I really liked her. Katherine was about my age, but she had a youthfulness to her, and she had reddish-brown hair that was clearly touched up, I mean there was no gray in it, and I wondered how she had kept it so nice during the pandemic. She was not a big person, and there was a litheness to her as she got up to throw away something in the trash can nearby, and then she came back and sat down again.

As we talked, Katherine Caskey spoke of her childhood. She had spent the first six years of her life in West Annett, she said, a town about an hour away, a small town; her father had been the minister there, and her mother had died when Katherine was just five. She spoke of her mother at length that evening, and I understood: This was Katherine's wound. She had loved her mother dearly, and her mother had adored her. And then her mother died. Her father tried to hold things together; Katherine's baby sister, Jeannie, had been sent to live with their father's mother in Shirley Falls, and Katherine and her father struggled along with a housekeeper named Connie Hatch. "Oh, I *hated* her," Katherine said, shaking her head. "That poor woman. I just hated her because she had a big birthmark on her nose, and she frightened me."

Katherine went on to say that the church congregants had started vicious rumors about her father and Connie—which had been ludicrous, of course—and that her father had broken down in front of the congregation one day—Katherine was in Sunday school and didn't see this, but all the kids talked of it for days to come: her father weep-

ing in front of his congregation. And then the congregation realized they had gone too far, and—according to
Katherine—they apologized to her father, though he still
left the place six months later.

"But here's what happened to poor Connie," Katherine
said, and her eyes widened, they were green eyes, and she
said, shaking her head so slowly, "Lucy, she murdered people at the county farm."

"She *did*?" I was about to take a sip from my plastic
cup of wine, but I put it back down.

"Yup. A few old people who were paralyzed. She suf-
focated them. To relieve their suffering, she said. And then
she went to prison, and my father would go visit her
there." Katherine gazed at me as she said this.

"You're kidding," I said.

"She died there."

"Oh my *God*!" I said. And Katherine agreed that it was
a terrible story.

Bob, I had noticed this, had stopped eating as Katherine
was talking. Half a lobster roll sat in front of him on the
waxy paper it had come in. When Katherine finally
stopped talking he said to her, "Your father was the minister? In West Annett?"

And Katherine said, "Uh-huh."

"Did you live in a farmhouse out in the middle of nowhere?" Bob asked. His mask was off, because he had been eating, and his face had taken on a strange look of almost wonder.

"We did!" Katherine said, turning toward him. "It was an awful old farmhouse that had been left to the church, and they made it the rectory."

"Hold on," Bob said. He reached into his pocket for his cellphone and poked a number, then, putting the phone to his ear, he said to Katherine, "What was your father's name?"

"Tyler. Tyler Caskey," said Katherine. I thought she seemed pleased that Bob had asked about her father.

Bob stood up and said into his phone, "Susie, it's me. Listen—" And he walked away from the table. Katherine looked at me with raised eyebrows. After a minute Bob was pushing another number and I heard him say, "Jimmy?" And then he walked farther away. But very shortly he returned to the table and he sat down, and he seemed almost breathless, and he said, "Katherine Caskey, I know who you are. Your father did my father's funeral, my father died when I was four, and the minister in Shirley Falls was on the outs with my mother, no idea why, and she drove to West Annett to find your father and he did the funeral. But, Katherine, that was you on the porch! You were standing there next to your father the entire time, and I never forgot you. Katherine, that was *you*?"

And here was something funny. She kept looking at him and looking at him. She had a strange look on her face, and then she said, "You were in the backseat next to a little girl."

"Yes!" Bob said. "My sister, Susan. And my brother was sitting in the front seat and my mother was rude to your father, I mean she was agitated because her husband had just died—"

"It's *you*—" Katherine said this quietly. "Oh my God, that was *you*."

"You remember? Seriously?"

"Oh my God, I do. I never, ever forgot that little boy in my entire life. You looked so sad, and we kept staring at each other."

Bob almost yelped. "I can't be*lieve* you remember that! Because I have *always* remembered that little girl who stood there and stared at me with her big eyes. I felt, I don't know—I felt like we were connected."

Katherine had now turned fully toward Bob, who was straddling the picnic table bench. "Well, we were," she said. "We *were* connected! Because we had both just lost a parent."

"I just called my siblings and Susan couldn't remember

but Jim said, Yes, the guy was from West Annett, and he remembered we went there, and he remembered my mother yelling at your father. But your father did the funeral anyway."

"I don't remember her yelling at my father. I just remember watching you." Katherine looked over at me; her face was filled with awe. And she looked back at Bob. "Oh my God," she said again, quietly. She shook her head slowly, and then she turned to where her husband was sitting at the picnic table near us, and she yelled, "Honey! Honey, *this* is the little boy I told you about!" But her husband was talking to William and Margaret, and Katherine turned back to Bob and said, "I can't believe this. I honestly can't believe this. We've known each other for a few years now, but it was *you* all along."

Slowly I began to understand what had happened, and a warmth moved through me.

Katherine said, "Bob Burgess, when this pandemic is over, I'm going to hug you so hard, I can't *tell* you how hard I am going to hug you."

"I look forward to that," Bob said, emotion moving over his face.

"How did your father die?" Katherine asked him then, and Bob told her the story of his father being hit by the car with his kids in it as he walked down the driveway to check the mail.

"Oh," Katherine said. "Oh Bob, I'm so sorry."

He even told her the part where Jim had confessed to him years later that he, Jim, was the one who had done it, who had fiddled with the gearshift, and how hard that had been for Bob, because he had—all his life—thought he was the one responsible for it. Katherine watched him with her green eyes. Then she said simply, "I'm so sorry about that, Bob. But I cannot believe it was you that I saw in the backseat of that car so many years ago. I *found* you." She shook her head slowly.

Bob bit into his lobster roll. "I know," he said, his mouth full. "I know."

So there was that kind of thing that happened. There were these times, is what I am saying, where the people I met were interesting. And their stories interwove! I was so glad for those two that night. When I told William, he did not seem impressed. He said, "They could be making it up. There are a lot of memories people have that aren't accurate."

I thought about this, and I remembered certain things from my own childhood that stood out as clearly to me as any memory: I remember my brother being beaten up on the playground one day; he was crouching with his hands to his ears and a few boys were kicking him. I had run away when I saw this, I mean I had run away from my brother and those boys. And there was another memory I had too, of my brother and my mother; that memory was too painful for me to think about—it only flashed through my mind. I didn't bother to answer William. I was just happy for Bob. And for Katherine Caskey too.

ii

There was a streak of good weather, and William and I would go exploring in the car. We had our Maine plates on again and we drove along small roads that wound around and ended up always by the ocean. I had traveled through tiny roads in Italy and Croatia, many different parts of Europe I had been to with my career, but this was like nothing I had ever seen, and I thought: It's so American. Because it was.

We went by old cemeteries and we stopped at one and read the names and dates on the headstones. William, walking ahead of me, said, "Lucy, look at this." And I went to where he was standing, he swept his arm, and I saw that there were a number of tombstones that had death dates in 1918 and 1919, and they were not always old people who had died. "The flu epidemic," William said to me.

And I thought: The world has been through this before.

It seemed far away, remote, yet for those who had friends and family die in the flu epidemic, it was as distressing to them as what we were living through now.

But we went exploring, is what I am saying, and the weather grew increasingly better. There was a sense of the physical world opening its hand to us, and it was beautiful. And it helped.

~

I looked up the flu epidemic on my computer and saw that the schools had been closed and also the churches. There were old photos of many people—usually men—lying on low-to-the-ground beds in makeshift hospitals.

William said to me, "Maybe someone in your family died in the flu epidemic. Want me to get you a subscription to an online ancestry thing?" He had a look of almost excitement as he asked me this.

I said, No. I did not want to know anything about my family.

iii

But I was sad because of the girls, I missed them almost constantly, and when we spoke they never said, "I miss you, Mom." I thought suddenly of how often Becka would say that to me even when she was married to Trey. But she did not say it these days.

Some mornings I woke even before William did, and I would take my walk because I was so anxious. And I was anxious because of the girls. One day I called Chrissy and asked her how Becka was doing—I knew she would tell Becka I had done this, but I wanted to know—and Chrissy said, "Mom, don't worry about her. She's got her shrink, Lauren, and she's got Michael and me, and she's doing okay."

"She doesn't call me anymore," I said.

Chrissy hesitated before she said, "I think she doesn't need you like she used to. Even those years married to Trey she still needed you, but, Mom, you did your job. She's on her way."

"Okay," I said. "I hear you."

And I did.

But it sort of killed me, I will tell you that.

~

Chrissy called me back two days later. She said, "Okay, now I have something to tell you, and it will make you happy. I didn't think we should talk about it in the same conversation about Becka." She said, "But I bet you already know."

"You're pregnant," I said.

The baby was due in December. "Don't tell Dad, I'm going to call him myself as soon as we hang up."

Oh, I was ecstatic—!

"He's out for his walk," I said. And we spoke about how she felt no sickness at all, just a slight queasiness at times, and she was eating like a horse. She said they were not going to know the sex of the child. "We want to be surprised." Then she said how glad she was that William had gotten rid of Melvin. "Can you *imagine,* Mom? I mean, I was pregnant that day, and if he had moved in with us— Oh Mom."

"I know," I said. "Are you still going to the protests?"

"Don't worry about the protests, Mom. They're small, and I stay really safe."

"Okay," I said. "Okay."

Oh, I was absolutely euphoric when we hung up! Chrissy was going to have her child! I thought about holding the baby and baby clothes and how Chrissy would be such a good mother; I pictured her with a boy, somehow, and— Oh, the whole thing just thrilled me!

. . .

And when William came back his face glowed as well; we spoke of it immediately. "She told you they're not going to learn the sex of it, right?" William asked, and I said, Yes, she had told me that. William said, "It's great, Lucy. This is great news." And I said I was so excited I could barely stand it.

And then not soon after I saw that William's face fell, and he said, "I miss Bridget." He walked over to look out at the water. He said, "I need to go see her again soon."

"Go anytime!" I said, but he did not answer me.

~

That night William was tapping on his computer, and he looked up and then closed it. He said to me, "Do you remember how when we wrote the vows for our wedding, you asked that we put in not just 'until death do us part,' but the words 'forever and beyond'? Do you remember that?"

"Remind me," I said.

"I just did." He looked over at the fireplace and then down at his shoe. "You wanted to make sure that it wasn't only until death do us part. You wanted to make sure that it was longer than that."

And then I did remember. I said, "I guess I'm afraid of death."

"I don't think so," William said. "I think you just really loved me and wanted it to go on forever." He said then, "I think it's the opposite of being afraid of death. I think you just don't believe in death."

"Of course I do," I said.

"Oh, I know in the real sense, but you— Oh, never mind," he said, as though suddenly exhausted. But then he said, waving a hand laconically, "You're a *spirit*, Lucy. You know things. I've told you that before. There is no one else out there like you."

I thought: He is wrong, I am scared of death. And I do not know anything.

iv

Protesters still went out into the streets every night and I still worried about their health, but the violence seemed to be over. When I asked the girls they said there had never been violence at the vigils or protests they attended in New Haven.

I listened carefully to people on the news, people of color, who said that every day they had to worry when they got into their cars that they could be stopped, or when they walked down the sidewalks in their neighbor-

hoods that they could be stopped. How they were con-
scious every single minute of being in real danger.

And it reminded me of how, many years earlier, after I
had left William, I went to a writers' conference in Ala-
bama, and there was a woman there, a poet, and she was
Black, and she had driven down from Indiana alone to
attend this conference, and she had gotten lost and it was
nighttime before she found where we were to stay at the
college. And what I suddenly remembered was her fear
that night. She had said to me, "You don't want to be a
Black woman alone on some desolate road down here."

I thought about that for a long time.

~

It was not long after this that my sister, Vicky, called me. I
was surprised when I saw her number show up on my
phone; she never called me but always waited for me to
call her, which I did once a week, as I have said.

Vicky said to me, "Lucy, I've joined a church."

I said, "You *have*?"

And she said, Yes, she had joined—and I cannot remember the name of it, but I recognized right away that it
was a Christian fundamentalist church—and she said it
had changed her life.

"In what way?" I asked her.

And Vicky said, "I know you'll be snotty about this, Lucy. But when you really pray—and when you pray with other people—the spirit of the Lord can honest and truly come to you."

So I said, "You mean you've seen the light?"

And Vicky said, "I knew you'd be sarcastic, I knew you would. I don't know why I even told you."

"I'm not being sarcastic!" I said. I was sitting on the lumpy red couch and I stood up as I said this. I walked around the room as she talked. She said she had joined two months ago, that she had never been in the presence of people so kind, and so I made another mistake and I said, "You're attending services with people? Vicky, there's a pandemic."

And Vicky said, "The Lord will protect me."

"But are you wearing masks?" I asked.

"We don't wear masks at church, Lucy. I have to wear one when I work, but at church we do not wear them. It's the government trying to force us to do that, Lucy. And I know you think differently, but you are being fooled."

I closed my eyes for a second and said, "Where are you getting your news from?"

She paused and then said, "Lucy, I have watched you on so many TV shows over the years, all those morning shows. And I *believed* them. I believed what I saw, but now I don't anymore. It's all baloney."

This startled me, because—in a way—she was right. I had been struck by that increasingly over the years: that when I did a television show, how there was always something slightly false about it, the perkiness of the newscasters, the setting, the whole thing. And the fact that the station was always looking for what was called "a hook."

Vicky went on. "I don't watch television anymore. I don't believe they are telling us the truth. They are telling us their truth to try and sway us in the wrong direction. I'm not going to tell you where I get my news, but that's how I feel."

I waited a moment and then I asked, "You joined this church two months ago, and you're only now telling me?"

She said, "You're wondering why I didn't tell you? Honestly, Lucy, look at your response."

I was suddenly tired, and I sat down again. "I didn't mean to be rude," I told her.

"Well, you were rude," Vicky said. "But I forgive you."

I asked if her husband and daughter Lila had joined the church as well. "They have," Vicky said. "And it has made a lot of difference in our lives, I will tell you that. We used to not even eat together, but now we do every night, and we say grace, and it becomes a whole different experience."

"I'm glad," I said. "I'm glad to hear that you're all eating together."

Right before Vicky hung up, she said, "I'm praying for you, Lucy."

"Thank you," I said.

When I told William he just shrugged and said, "I hope it makes her happy."

~

I still walked, once in the morning and again in the after-noon. The old man who sat on his front steps smoking—Tom—we became friendlier. A bush by the steps was tilting toward his head as he sat there one day. "Tom," I said, "how are you?" And he said, "Doin' okay, de-ah. How about you?" There was not much to talk about, and so we talked about how there was not much to talk about. Then he said, "How're you liking the Winterbourne house?" And I said it was fine. His eyes went to the side for a moment, and when he looked back at me he said, "Well, I'm glad you're there." And then I suddenly understood that Bob Burgess might have been right about Tom put-ting that sign on our car months earlier, because of how Tom had specifically mentioned the Winterbourne place and the way his eyes had looked away for a moment. But I just said, "Well, thank you, Tom, that makes me glad."

As I turned to walk away, Tom said to me, squinting his

eyes against his cigarette smoke, "It makes my day to see you, de-ah. It always does."

I told him it was the very same for me.

V

And then this happened:

Toward the end of June, Becka got the virus.

Chrissy called to tell me this; it was midafternoon, and I was just getting ready for my walk. William was out looking at the guard tower. Chrissy said: "Mom, listen and don't freak out. *Please.*"

I said, "I won't freak out, but tell me."

And she told me that Becka had the virus; she had gotten it from Trey. Becka had gone back to Brooklyn to see him and they had sex. He said he had no idea that he had the virus, but he became sick the next day, and Becka became sick five days later.

I said, "*Chrissy.* I can't believe this!"

And Chrissy said, "I know."

When I hung up, I sat for a long while at the table, and then I called William, who was out for his walk. "I'll be home in five minutes," he said.

When he came through the door, he looked old to me, and I felt angry with Becka then. For just a few very brief moments, I felt angry with her. And then it passed. "You call her," I said, and William did. He was careful as he spoke to her. I heard her begin to cry, but she answered his questions. Her fever was not very high, she had no sense of taste or smell, and her lungs felt "spongey" as she took a shower. William reported this to me after he hung up. He also said she had asked, "Is Mom mad at me?" And that hurt my heart. He had told her no, that we were both just concerned. But William looked defeated as he sat there, his shoulders were slumped and his eyes were far away.

It's a funny thing. I was not as concerned about her having the virus as I was about the state of her marriage. What I mean is, I somehow felt right away that she was young and that she would be okay—and she was—but I was worried about her being back with Trey. And I also felt a sense of great weariness. William and I sat together silently for a long while. Through the window the bright green of the new leaves was picked up by the sun, you could almost see through the leaves, they were that fresh.

~

Becka called me the next day. She was calling from the bathroom and her voice was sort of muffled. "Mom, I'm so embarrassed, I'm so— Oh Mom," she said.

I listened to her as I walked around the little green lawn

area by the house. She told me that Trey had been calling her and that she had missed him, and that she wanted to get back with him. "But I didn't want to tell you." I said I understood. She said that Trey had told her it had ended— supposedly—with the other woman. "She's a poet too, Mom. *God*." I kept listening. But when Becka got back to their apartment, the reality of Trey wasn't what she had pictured. "Mom, he's gross. But we had sex, Mom. I don't know why—but we had sex, and it sort of seemed right then, but not really— Oh *Mom*."

I let her go on until she ran down, and then I told her it was not a new story, these things happened all the time between couples who were trying to decide what to do.

"Seriously?" she asked.

"Oh, seriously," I said. I did not say that her father and I had played this out similarly—in our own way—when we were splitting up.

I just let her continue to talk, and she talked until she got tired, but it was a long time before she hung up.

After Trey got better—he got better faster than Becka did—he moved into some apartment on the Lower East Side. And Becka stayed in their apartment. William had bought it for them when they got married. "I want to sell it," Becka said, and William told her to slash the price and get out of there. As soon as Becka got better—it took her more than three weeks—she put the place on the market and went back to Connecticut to live in the guesthouse near Michael and Chrissy.

vi

For some reason that I did not understand, it continued to bother me to think of my apartment in New York. I kept thinking: Go away. I felt that it tugged on my heart almost constantly, but not in a good way, and I saw that more and more time would go by before I would be there, and when I pictured finally walking back into the place—and when would that be?—it filled me with a kind of despair. David would not be there. But he had not been there for a year before this whole pandemic. I did not know what to do. And there was nothing to do anyway. *Mom,* I cried silently to the nice mother I had made up, *Mom, I am so confused!* And the nice mother I had made up said, I know you are, Lucy. But it will work out. You just hang tight, honey, that's all you need to do.

~

Not long after Becka returned to Connecticut, she called me with excitement in her voice. She had met a friend of

Michael's, he had also already had the virus, and so they had seen each other a number of times. "I think he likes me," Becka said.

"Of course he likes you," I said. Then I asked, "What does he do?"

"He's a screenwriter," Becka said. "He does documentaries."

And I thought: Oh dear God. He will break her heart because this is so often what happens in first relationships after a separation or divorce. But I did not tell her that.

vii

Chrissy lost her baby.

She had gone out for a short run and developed cramps and then when she got home she was bleeding so badly that Michael drove her to the emergency room. She spent the day there; they'd managed to stop the bleeding and she was home now.

Becka was the one who called and told me, and she said, "Don't feel bad, but she can't talk to you right now." I said I understood. But I thought: *Chrissy! Oh dear Chrissy!* "But how is she?" I asked this quietly. And Becka paused and then said, "Well, she's how you would expect, Mom. She's really upset."

"Of course," I said.

We spoke for a few more minutes; I asked her to have Michael call me when he could, and Becka said she would do that. And then we hung up.

I sat at the round dining room table, stupefied. Again and again I thought, Oh Chrissy, Chrissy.

Chrissy.

When William got back to the house, I told him. He sat across from me at the table and he didn't say anything. We just sat there for a very long time, not speaking. Finally I said, "Why would she go for a *run*?"

William opened his hand that was on the table and said, "The doctor told her she could keep running."

"He did?" I asked. "Why?"

William only shook his head.

"But how do you know the doctor said that?" I persisted.

"She told me one day. She told me the doctor had said she could keep up with her exercise for now." William stood up and walked over to the living room window, then came back and sat down across from me again.

And then I remembered that when I was young, my mother had said—about some woman in our town who had adopted a child, and the child had not turned out all right—my mother had said, "When a woman can't have a baby, there's a reason." She meant because the woman would not be a good mother.

And it horrified me as I recalled this, because I had sort of believed it.

But Chrissy would be a wonderful mother. When I spoke of it to William, he rolled his eyes and said, "Your mother was an absolute whack job. God, Lucy."

I thought about this.

My mother, because she was my mother, had great gravity in my young life. In my whole life. I did not know who she was, and I did not like who she had been. But she was my mother, and so some part of me had continued to believe things she had said.

~

The days went by, but I do not really remember how. The silence from Chrissy made me feel numb with awfulness. Michael finally called, and he sounded very serious. He said, "She's hurting." And I said, Of course.

And then, one day toward the end of the week, William came back from his walk and said, "I just talked to both of them. They have the virus."

Apparently Chrissy had gotten it at the emergency room, because the next day she received a phone call and was told that unfortunately she had been in the presence of someone who tested positive, but because she had her mask on she would probably be all right. But she was not all right. And then Michael became ill as well. Michael's symptoms were different, he had an extreme backache but, bizarrely, not terrible trouble with his asthma, although there was some. Chrissy's symptoms were more like Becka's had been.

I called Becka immediately and she picked up. She said, "They're going to be okay, Mom. Don't worry. I'm here taking care of them." And I told her I was proud of her, and she said—with just the slightest sound of disgust, it seemed to me—"Of course."

"William," I said. "Why did they call you but not me?" I did not feel jealous of him, I simply wanted to know.

And he said, "Oh Lucy, they just worry about how much you worry."

"But aren't you worried about them? About Michael?"

"Yes," William said, "but I don't let it show."

"I get it," I said, and I did.

~

Chrissy eventually called me the next week and she sounded quiet. I asked her how she felt and she said she was okay, she was getting better, and Michael was too. It was strange, she said, that Michael had only had a little bit of extra trouble with his breathing, but he was getting better, though she said he had had "brain fog."

"Oh God," I said, and she said, "Yeah, he said he has a peek into what dementia could be like." I thought: Sweet Jesus. "But it's getting better," she said. "It's definitely getting better."

Then Chrissy said, "We are going to have a kid, Mom. One way or another we are going to have a family."

And I said, "Yes, you will."

Chrissy said, "That guy that Becka liked—the documentary writer. He turned out to be a douchebag and she's feeling pretty bad."

"Oh God," I said.

"She'll get over it," Chrissy said, and I said she was right.

When we hung up I was aware that I felt a slight sense of remove from both the girls, and I understood this was because their sadness affected me too much.

Three

i

William had stayed in touch with Lois Bubar, his half-sister, and now that it was July they had come up with a plan. They would each drive two and a half hours and meet on the campus of the University of Maine, in Orono. He read me her emails—almost obsessively, it seemed to me—and she'd suggested this plan after he'd said that he was so Covid-averse he could not stay in her house, which she had initially invited him to do; he had said it nicely, and she had responded with the Orono plan. He told her that I would not be coming with him, though not out of any hostility, and she wrote back that she understood perfectly, that she was very much looking forward to meeting him.

"I have to take her something," William said, a few days before he was to make the trip. "What can I take her, Lucy?"

"We'll figure it out," I said, but I had no idea what he should take her.

The next day he said to me, "I'm going to make her brownies."

"Brownies?" I asked.

"Yes," he said. "I have never made brownies before, but I'm going to make them for her."

"Okay," I said.

He went to the grocery store and came back with a tinfoil brownie pan and a box of brownie mix. I watched him as he stirred up the dark brown stuff and spread it in the pan; he had already smooshed a lot of butter over the bottom of the pan. He put the pan into the oven, and I said, "Check it five minutes earlier than it says, this oven is old." And he did, but the edges of the brownies were already a little burned, and he looked crestfallen.

"They're perfect," I said. "I'm telling you, William, this is perfect." I put a sheet of tinfoil over the top.

In the morning William packed a lunch and took some bottles of water, and he left early.

It was not an especially hot day, the sky was very blue, but there were lots of white clouds as well, and so I called Bob Burgess and asked if he wanted to go for a walk. "Or Margaret too," I added. But Margaret was busy, and so Bob drove up, and we walked toward the cove, and I told him the whole story of Lois Bubar—I had told him some of it before, but this time I went into great detail—and he kept watching me and saying, "Lucy! Wow!" I loved how much he paid attention, how much he cared. "So I'm very nervous and hope it goes well," I said.

"I'm nervous myself now," Bob said.

Then I told him how Chrissy had lost her baby, and—I am not kidding you—Bob stopped walking and his eyes above his mask became wet. "Oh Lucy," he said quietly. I told him it was the second miscarriage she had had, and he just repeated "Oh Lucy." And I said, Thank you, Bob. And then we kept walking. The sun was high in the blue sky, white clouds were puffy near it, and then, in a single moment, the sun went behind one of the clouds and it changed the way the world looked; I mean the road we walked on, the trees, became softer.

I said to him, "My sister found God."

And here's what was so interesting to me. He looked at me, really looked at me, and then he nodded just slightly and said, "I get it." And I said, "Thanks. Because I do too." The sun came back out and then we reached the cove.

Sitting on the bench, Bob said, "So, Lucy, do you believe in God?"

I was amazed. Nobody I knew had ever asked me such a thing. So I told him the truth. I said, "Well, I don't *not* believe in God." I squinted out over the cove, the water had a splash of white light on it from the sun, and there were a few seagulls at one of the wharfs. And I said, "I mean I don't believe in a father-type God—like my sister does—" And Bob said, "You don't know if your sister believes in a father-type God," and I looked at him and said, "No, you're right, I didn't ask her." Bob said, "Go on, though, I'm curious to know your thoughts." So I said, "Well, my feelings about God have shifted over the years, and all I can say is: There's more than meets the eye." I added, "I'm just pretty sure there's more than meets the eye."

Bob was watching me. He had lit a cigarette and was just holding it in front of him. "What *I* think," he said, "is what was written on a huge sheet of paper that was tacked onto the bulletin board in the Congregational church we sometimes went to when I was a kid. GOD IS LOVE. That was written in block letters on this bulletin board in the downstairs reception room. And it's so funny that I would remember it, but I guess I always have." He inhaled, squinting against the smoke.

"Well, that's a good thing to remember," I said. "It's true." After a moment I said, "You know, I read a book a few years ago, and some character in it said something like, It's our duty to bear the burden of the mystery with as much grace as we can."

Bob nodded. "That's pretty good."

I said, "Yeah, I thought so too."

It seemed we had nothing more to say about this, and so we sat in companionable silence for quite a while as he smoked and the sun shone down. Then Bob asked, "Remember when we used to read newspapers? Real ones?" And I said, "Yes, the Sunday *Times* was kind of given the whole morning." Then I said, "Why did you ask that?" And he shrugged and said, "I miss it, that's all. I miss the everyday part of it, the reading of all sorts of things I didn't know about. I mean every so often I *do* buy the paper, but it's so much easier to just get the news on my computer."

I sat forward and told Bob about a lecture I had heard maybe ten years ago at Columbia University about the internet and all the changes it was bringing. I told him how this lecturing man said that there had been three major revolutions in the history of man's world: the first, the agricultural revolution; the second, the industrial revolution; and the third was this social revolution—meaning the way the internet was changing the world. I said, "And what I most remember was that this guy told us that—because we are in the middle of it—we will not live long enough to see how it plays out in this world." I told Bob that it made me think of my sister and how she got her news probably on the internet in places I would never think to go to.

And Bob, who was squishing out his cigarette on the side of the bench, said, "Yeah, you make a good point. I think how the internet has made so many things—good and bad—possible." He stuck the cigarette butt back in the cigarette pack, which is what he always did.

As we stood up to start our walk back, I said, "William told me about his prostate, and I want to thank you for getting him to your doctor for his blood tests. That was so good of you."

"Well, sure" is all Bob said.

I almost said, Talk about God being love! But I did not say that.

When we got back to the house before he got into his car, he opened his arms and said "Big hug to you, Lucy," and I opened my arms and said "And to you too, Bob."

~

It was seven o'clock by the time William pulled into the driveway.

He came—almost—bounding into the house, he had taken his mask off on the way to the house, and he said, "Lucy! She's wonderful! Lucy, she loves me!" This is what he said, with his big brown eyes positively shining, and oh dear God I was so glad.

. . .

I said I would cook that night so that he could tell me everything. And so he sat at the table and spoke more rapidly than I could ever remember him speaking. "I have a *sister*!" He kept saying this, and shaking his head. "Lucy, I have a *sister*." He told me they had met on the steps of the library, that they recognized each other immediately "not only because we were the only two old people on the steps" but because they *recognized* each other. Even with their masks on. "The minute I saw her, I thought, It's you!" And he told me that she had said the exact same thing. And so they took their lawn chairs and sat on the large area of grass in front of the library, and they talked and talked and talked.

Lois said that she had gone to the university, that all her kids had gone there, and that her eldest grandson had graduated from there two years ago June. She said that she'd met her husband there, and then he had gone to Tufts for dental school. She said that her youngest brother, Dave, ran the Trask farm—the potato farm—she had grown up on, with his son, Joe. And then she asked about William's daughters, she was especially kind about poor Bridget being stuck with her mother's loser boyfriend, she had been so *nice* about that, and when William told her about Chrissy's miscarriages, he said to me, "Lucy! She got tears in her eyes! She said she had miscarried twice and she felt just awful for Chrissy."

. . .

And then they talked about their mother, Catherine Cole. Over and over they went on about what Catherine had come from, and why she had married Lois's father, and why she had left him for the German, as Lois referred to William's father.

I sat watching William from across the table. In all the years I had known the man, I did not think I had ever seen him so happy.

Only later that night, as I lay awake, did I realize that William had been lonely. In spite of me, and our girls, and Bridget, and his other two wives, William had felt alone in the world. And now he had a sister. Inside myself I wept. From happiness and sadness both.

And then right before I fell asleep a thought went through my mind: that William had chosen to come to Maine during the pandemic because he had a sister here. He must have been hoping this would happen, a resolution between them. Otherwise he would have taken me to a house in Montauk. But we had come to Maine.

Could that be true? I wondered this as I fell asleep.

ii

I began to think that my mind was not right.

I could not remember things. I would start a sentence and then not remember where I was going with it. Bob said, "That happens to me too. I think it's just Covid mind."

But it did not go away. If anything, I thought it might be getting worse. And there was also, in my head, a sense of confusion. When I walked into my bedroom, for example, I would think: Now, why did I come in here? It made me think of Michael and his "brain fog" that had come with the virus, but his brain fog had gone away, and I did not have the virus. But honestly, there were times I could not remember why I had walked into some room. And in the kitchen, making coffee, for example, I thought that my motions were slower as I placed the filter into the coffee machine. It was disconcerting: I felt old.

I mentioned it to William and he didn't seem to have any response. I said, "But have you noticed?"

And he said, waving his hand, "You're fine, Lucy."

I did not feel fine.

~

One evening I watched something on my computer. It was about physics and how we have no free will. I watched it, feeling that I could not understand it that well, but I sort of—a little bit—understood what they were saying when they said that all things have already happened, that there is no past or present or future. That interested me. I asked William what he thought—I explained it to him after I'd watched it—and as I explained it I remembered how the previous summer in Maine, going to find his half-sister, he had said to me one night that very seldom did people *choose* to do anything; they just did it.

Now he looked at me from his chair across the room—he had been reading a book—and shrugged. "I'm not a physicist, Lucy."

"I know, but what do you *think*?"

He shifted his legs. "I think they could be right. But so what." Then he said, "It kind of explains your mother's visions, though."

"I know," I said, "I thought the same thing. But what do you mean 'So what'? Seriously, William, this is interesting to me. If everything is predetermined, then"—and I looked around the room—"what are we doing here?"

There was a small smile that came to half of his mouth, but he looked tired. "I know. I think that sometimes."

"But what *are* we doing here?" I persisted.

"What I'm doing here, Lucy," he said, "is I'm trying to

save your life." He paused and then said, "But think if you had gone to Italy and Germany for your book tour like you were supposed to. You might be dead. And you just didn't go."

"I know. For no reason," I said.

"I know that." He picked up his book again. "No past or present or future. It's interesting, I agree with you." But then he shrugged and said, "Who the hell knows anything, Lucy." And he started to read again.

iii

I dyed my hair. I have had my hair colored with blond highlights for years, but now my hair was coming in brown—with only a few wisps of gray—and when my hair is brown I feel that I look like my mother, which is a thing I cannot bear. So I went to the drugstore and looked at the packages of color, and I chose one and came home and followed the directions, and within two hours my hair was back to being blond. It had come out perfectly!

And then my hair began to fall out.

The bathtub drain became plugged up, and I would stand in water above my ankles, and it would take hours for the water to drain. It was an old bathtub, and the drain was one that could not be removed. It could only open—about half an inch—and close. Each time I took a shower the water took longer to drain out of the tub, and after it did the tub was filthy.

And my hair! I kept tying it up, but it was so thin it was ghastly. A friend in New York suggested pills to order on-line to make it grow, and so I did, but the pills upset my stomach terrifically. After a while it stopped falling out, and it just lay limply against my neck.

I finally told William that we had to get a plumber in, and he said no plumber was coming into the house because of the virus. So he looked online and read that if you put half a box of baking soda into the drain and then a cup of white vinegar, it would solve the problem.

The next morning William lay half crunched up inside that bathtub on a dirty towel, trying to slip baking soda into the little half-inch opening. He kept swearing, and finally he was sticking the baking soda in with a knife down the little slit. It took him a really long time, and when he climbed out of the tub he said, wiping himself off, "It's all yours now, Lucy." So I poured in a cup of vinegar and it sort of sizzled a bit, but the water still did not go down.

William was disgusted and went for his walk.

I poured a gallon of the white vinegar down the drain then and listened to it gurgle more, and then I looked on-line and I poured a gallon of bleach in as well—

And it worked! I could not wait for William to get home, so I called him and said, "It worked."

"It *did*?" he said, and when he came home, honestly we were as excited as kids who had succeeded in starting a fire by rubbing two sticks together. The drain worked perfectly and I was glad then to clean the tub.

My hair remained blond but very, very thin.

As time went by my hair became brown again and I told myself: Well, at least it is growing out, but it grew back in odd ways and wouldn't lie flat on my head. *Mom,* I said silently to the nice mother I had made up, *Mom, I look awful!* And the nice mother I had made up said, It's okay, Lucy. Your hair has gone through a shock.

And I understood that to be true. At first it was hard to look at myself in the mirror. But I got used to it. I thought: Who cares.

(But I cared.)

iv

We took the plexiglass off the porch and put up the screens that were leaning against the inside wall. We ate out there—the porch was large enough for the round dining room table with its flowered tablecloth and the pompoms on it, if we put one leaf down. And the ocean was immense; we could hear it at night now with the windows open. I learned this about the sound of the sea: There were two levels to it, there was a deep ongoing sound that was quietly massive, and there was also the sound of the water hitting the rocks; always this was thrilling to me. The light was astonishing, it would come every morning and it would be a pale white and then almost smash into a yellow, and then it seemed to get even more yellow as the day went by. When it rained it was not a really cold rain, although most nights the air would get colder.

～

A strange compatibility was taking place gradually between William and me. I had even forgotten about how I used to have to go down to the water and swear because he wasn't listening to me when we had supper. I mean, we were essentially stuck together, and we sort of adapted to it. We would talk about the different people we met, and I told him one evening about a woman named Charlene Bibber that I had met that day at the food pantry—Margaret had asked me to fill in for a day when a volunteer couldn't make it.

. . .

And so I had gone to the place, it was a wooden building, not terribly large, and there were five of us volunteering. We were to pack the boxes and grocery bags, and we stood six feet apart with our masks on and put canned foods and toilet paper and diapers, and some frozen meat, into boxes, and then we put produce into paper bags: The produce had come mostly from the grocery store in town, and the lettuce and the celery looked a little worn out, but we did this, and the idea was that when the people arrived to get it—Margaret said that the pantry fed about fifty families—we would take it out to their cars.

I found myself toward the end of a table, and one woman pushed over a rolling cart with canned goods on it, and she stood next to me; the way the room was shaped we were almost in a separate area, and this woman said that her name was Charlene Bibber. I knew she was a volunteer because she wore the blue smock that all the volunteers wore. She started to talk to me quietly, almost without stopping. She had wavy hair with a little gray in it, and her nose was small, it turned up just slightly; I saw this when her mask slipped down. She told me right away that she was fifty-three years old. As she put the canned foods into the boxes she told me this part: She worked as a cleaner at the Maple Tree Apartments, a retirement place in town. She had been laid off for three weeks because of the virus, but then they let the cleaners go back.

Charlene said, tugging her mask back up, that her husband had died years earlier, and that she had never been able to have children. As I glanced at her face above her mask, she told me that she had never got over the death of her husband. She said that she had gone to a minister—she did not say what church—and the minister had said to her, "You get up every day and you put a smile on your face. That's what I do."

Charlene looked over at me. "How dumb was that?" she asked, and I said it was dumb. Then Charlene said, speaking even more quietly, that she had had a "fling"—that's how she put it—after her husband had died with a fellow in town named Fergie, and then he died and his wife had ended up living in the Maple Tree Apartments, and Charlene had stolen her shoe. One shoe. "I was going to give it back the next week, but then we got laid off for three weeks," she said. No one else seemed to be listening to us speak, and she went on. "I lied about it too, because when I showed up the next week, they told me that the woman—Ethel MacPherson—had said I had stolen her shoe, and I said, Oh, she's going batty, and they all had a laugh about it, I mean the women in the front office, and then they said I had to take a leave, I mean all the cleaners did—there are four of us—because of the virus. And when we went back after three weeks, Ethel had died."

I thought about this. "Why *one* shoe?" I asked. I was really curious.

Charlene nodded and said, "Because the first woman I cleaned for that morning—her name is Olive Kitteridge, and she was just sitting in her chair like a big bullfrog—and then Olive said, 'I've been sitting here thinking about a young woman that I stole one shoe from once.' And I asked her why one shoe, and she turned and said to me, 'I thought it might make her feel crazy.' And I said, Did it? And Olive shrugged and said, 'Dunno.'"

I liked this woman, Charlene Bibber.

When we walked the bags and boxes out to the waiting cars, most of the people who were driving the cars were women. Some had children in their cars. And the children looked at me and then looked away. And I understood. Some of the women were very grateful, but most of them just took the food and said "Thanks" and drove away. And I understood that too.

As we left the place for the day, I saw that on Charlene's car was a bumper sticker for the current president of our country. I thought that was fascinating, it intrigued me, really.

. . .

When I told William about Charlene, and mentioned the bumper sticker, he said "Huh," as though really considering it. "You don't think about his supporters working at a food pantry, but of course they can—and do." He looked at me. "Jesus, look at how small-minded I am."

And I said, "Yes, exactly." I said, "I think we don't get it. I mean, obviously we don't get it—their point of view."

And he said, "*I* get it."

I was surprised. "Tell me," I said.

And William crossed one leg over the other and said, "They're angry. Their lives have been hard. Look at your sister, Vicky. She's working a dangerous job right now, because she has to. But she still can't get ahead." Then he said, "Lucy, people are in *trouble*. And those who aren't in trouble, they just don't get it. Look how *I* just didn't get it—being surprised that this Charlene woman was working in a food pantry. And also, we make the people who *are* in trouble feel stupid. It's not good."

V

Along those lines, this is important, I think:

I need to tell you about one summer evening: William

and I took a drive after we ate dinner—it was still light out—and we stopped at a roadside place that was selling ice cream. The place that sold the ice cream was a small blue shack with a lot of lawn around it, and a tree stood in the middle of the lawn. When we first got there, people—not many—were milling about on the lawn, and we got out of our car and stood in line, at a safe distance from the woman ahead of us, who wore no mask. The woman who was serving the ice cream was not a young woman and she wore a mask but she wore it below her nose, and I wondered if William would say we shouldn't get ice cream from her, but he said nothing, and this is what I want to say:

An old man with a white beard was sitting on a stool beneath the tree, playing the guitar and singing a song, and there was another man, who had just gotten his ice cream, even I could tell immediately that he was from out of state, maybe even New York, and the car he got into was expensive-looking and slung low to the ground, but I could not see the license plates. This man wore dark pink shorts and a blue collared shirt tucked into them, and he wore loafers with no socks, and I heard behind me some people speaking of him. "Fucking out-of-stater." And I turned and they were men who wore no masks who had said that, and they looked a little frightening to me. And then the woman ahead of me in line—who was not wearing a mask—saw another woman who got out of her car, and they threw their arms around each other and said, "*Hi!*"

What I am trying to say is that for a few minutes I had what almost felt like a vision: that there was deep, deep unrest in the country and that the whisperings of a civil war seemed to move around me like a breeze I could not quite feel but could sense. We got our ice cream and we left, and I told William what I had felt and he said, "I know."

It has stayed with me. That feeling I had that evening.

~

In the toy chest one day we found beneath some rags two fire engines that were kind of incredible. I mean they were each about a foot long and made of metal, and had rubber tires; they seemed very old but in good shape because they had been made so well, and one had a metal ladder on the back that still worked. "Look at these," William said. He was sort of blown away by them, and I did not blame him; it seemed they had been made back at a time when toys were taken really seriously. He cleaned them off and put them on the windowsills of the porch, these two old toy fire engines from days far gone by.

Four

i

One night as we ate our supper I said, "William, how's your tower?" I said this sort of jokingly, but he responded with seriousness.

"My tower, as you put it," he said, glancing at me with his eyebrows raised, "built to watch for German submarines, is there as a reminder to me every day of what this world went through, and how it can go through that again." I waited, and he continued. "This country is in so much trouble, Lucy. The whole world is. It's like—" William put his fork down. "It's like some *seizure* is taking place around the world, and I'm just saying I think we're headed for real trouble. We are just tearing each other up. I don't know how long our democracy can work."

And I slowly understood that William's relationship to the tower was his relationship to our world as it was right now. He had connected the dots of history that I only vaguely, in my own way, was aware of.

He picked his fork up again and we ate in silence. Through the screens on the porch the sea stretched out before us, making its soft full sound so continuously, and there were the islands straight in front of us, with a lot more green on them now, and the water slapped against the rocks without stopping.

ii

Bob said that it was too hot for him to walk with me, but he still came over and we would sit on the lawn chairs, and sometimes Margaret came with him. If she was not with him he would have a cigarette, which he seemed to get such a kick out of. "Thank you, Lucy," he would say each time, and wink at me, his mask pulled down below his chin so he could smoke. With Bob, I was always okay-feeling. Even when I could not remember what I was going to say, he would just shrug and tell me, "Don't worry." I told him what William had said about our country—the world—being in trouble, and Bob said, "He may be right."

~

With William—he sometimes seemed so far away, and I remembered that this is how he had always been. But also,

I noticed—as I said—that I felt an increasing sense of comfort from how familiar he was becoming to me again. Still, I could never really settle into myself. Not for very long. Although it helped to have my music back, and there were those times when I would lie on the couch and listen to classical music on my phone.

But what scared me was that I could not—except when I was listening to the music—remember David in really concrete ways. He slipped and slid in my mind, like he would not hold still. I could not understand it.

iii

The girls called me far less frequently than—in my memory—they used to. I felt them moving away from me, and I knew I was not wrong. I did not understand why. It caused me at times a terrible private anguish. When I spoke to William about it he would shrug and say, "Lucy, let them be."

I remembered this: The last time I saw my mother, when I went to the hospital in Chicago where she was dying, I was on the phone with the girls at various points, they were in high school, and I worried about them, and my mother—who said almost nothing to me at all during the one night and the next morning that I was there—said this:

"You're too bound up with those girls. Watch out, they will end up biting you in the back."

She said that to me, my mother.

And the next morning she asked me quietly to leave. And I left.

But remembering this now, it frightened me. I thought: Did my mother have a vision? And I thought, No, she was only jealous of how much I loved my daughters. But maybe she had had a vision. And I was not the mother I thought I had been.

How will I ever know?

I think some people know. But I will never know.

~

But I missed them. Oh dear God did I miss those girls. I asked William when we could drive to Connecticut again and see them, and I said that Estelle and Bridget could drive over from Larchmont, and he said maybe one of these days, but not right now. So I let it go.

I had a memory of us standing in that driveway, and how we then sat around the pool, and it had been awkward. And as time went by, the idea of seeing the girls that way again was almost as bad as not seeing them at all.

But I also wondered why they did not offer to come up and see us. Both girls and Michael had already had the virus, surely they could drive up and see us, safe-distancing. When I mentioned to people how much I missed my girls, sometimes a person would say, Why can't they come up and see you? And I did not dare say: Because apparently they don't want to. And I was not going to ask them to come. That is not the kind of mother I am, *that* much I know.

iv

William was finding a new calling.

Lois's nephew—her brother Dave's son, called Joe— ran the Trask potato farm these days with his father. The potato farm had had trouble with parasites. William got very interested. He told me that the first time he called Lois's nephew, Joe referred to him as "Dr. Gerhardt." Joe spoke at great length with William about the University of Maine at Presque Isle, which had a program that was try- ing to help with this stuff. William spent a lot of time on the phone with Joe—who William said sounded like "a great fellow"—and he also spent time on the phone with other parasitologists he had worked with over the years who knew more about these particular parasites than William did. And William also researched. At dinner he would tell me about these parasites and what he was doing to help; he would go on and on, and to be truthful I was often made tired by this. But I was glad he was so involved in something. He seemed younger to me.

I felt older every day.

My mother—my real mother, not the nice mother I had made up—once said, "Everyone needs to feel important." And I thought of this as I listened to William go on about the potato parasites.

~

There was one night when Bob and Margaret invited us to a small gathering with one other couple at a place on the coast that was doing takeout. And so we went, and it was fine. Their friends were really nice, it seemed to me, and we had—I had—a pleasant enough time. But this is not the point.

The point is this: That as we drove home, we went through a part of town where I had not been. There were houses, intermittently through the outer town area, there were trees in front of them, and the houses were blue or gray or white, and as we drove by them it all seemed very quiet—it was a small town—and as we drove by these houses, it suddenly came to me with a terrible force: These were houses not unlike those I had driven past in my childhood. I would sometimes go to the neighboring towns of Hanston or Carlisle, Illinois, and—in my mind I was with my father—we would drive by these kinds of houses, and I remembered how once I saw a young couple by a house, they were all dressed up and their parents were out front taking photos of them, and I asked my father, Was it a wedding? And he said no, it was a school prom, and he added, "All foolishness. Total rubbish," he had said. And that night as William and I drove home from a perfectly pleasant evening, my insides collapsed and I felt that old, old desolation, because these were houses where people lived and did normal things, this is how I had seen it as a child and it is how I saw it now, and I said to William, "My whole childhood was a lockdown. I never saw anyone or went anywhere." And the truth of this hit me straight into the bowels, and William just looked at me and said, "I know, Lucy." He said it as a reflex, without thinking about what I had said, is what I thought.

. . .

But I was so sad that evening: I understood—as I have understood at different points in my life—that the childhood
isolation of fear and loneliness would never leave me.

My childhood had been a lockdown.

V

And then—that same night came my terrific panic attack.

It came to me as I tried to fall asleep—it was warm in my
little bedroom, and I could hear the ocean through my
skylight, which was now open, and also the window, but I
did not really hear it, because I was panicking. The panic
started as I pictured my apartment in New York, and it
seemed to me as I thought about it that I really did not
want to see it again. I could picture its emptiness; David
would never again come through the door, and whenever I
got back there I would have to walk into that apartment
alone. The thought of this felt unbearable.

And when I thought of my apartment, I remembered
that David had almost always been there. Because of his
bad hip, he did not go out for long walks, or to the gym
the way other men might have, he had always been there
except when he was at rehearsal or playing at the Philhar-

monic at night, and I thought of that now—that the apartment, it held no appeal for me.

I thought of David's cello where it sat in the corner of the bedroom in its case, and the thought of it disturbed me. It was almost off-putting, the image of his cello.

This frightened me. It petrified me, the idea that the apartment waiting for me in New York was not one I felt any genuine connection to—it made me panic in a way I had not panicked while this entire pandemic had been going on. I got up and went downstairs, and then out onto the porch, and then out onto the lawn, and the moon was almost full and I watched the water down below, the tide was coming in, and the water was lazily slapping at the rocks below me.

Mom, help me, I'm so scared!, I said to my made-up mother, but her answer—I know, Lucy, and I'm sorry—was weak. Oh dear God! I had made up everything in my life, I thought! Except for my girls, and maybe even them I had made up, I mean their graciousness to me and to each other, how did I know?

I turned around but my vision was blurry, and I could only see our house on this cliff, almost tilting in my mind, because I was so frightened. I sat down on the grass and said to myself, Lucy, stop this! But I could not stop, I kept picking at the grass and my hand was shaking.

Oh please help me, I thought, please please—but when you are really panicking there is no answer for it, and I knew that.

I wept, but not much, I cannot always cry.

I got up and went back inside, almost stumbling, and I could hear William coming out of the bathroom upstairs, and so I went quickly up the stairs and I said, "Pill, Pillie, oh God."

And he was on his way back to his room and he looked at me and he said, "Oh Lucy, you look so pretty."

He said that!

I said, "Are you crazy? I look like an old woman in a mug shot!"

And he said, "No, you look pretty, your hair is down and your little nightgown, but, Lucy, you've gotten far too thin."

And then he seemed to notice my distress, and he said, "Lucy, what is it?"

I went into his room and began to cry. To really, really cry. I said, "William, I am so homesick!"

And he started to be nice, but I said, "No, you don't understand, I have no home to go to!"

He said, "Of course you do, Lucy, you have your apartment—"

And I said, "No, no! You don't understand! It's a place

where I lived, and I loved David, but it was never a home. William, why wasn't it a home?" And then I said, "The only real home I ever had in my whole *life,* I had with you. And the girls." And I cried and cried. He opened his arms to me and brought me to sit with him on the bed. "Come here, Button," he said. "Sit on my lap," he said, and I did.

He held me very tightly. I had forgotten the strength of William's arms. It had been years since he had held me. And I said, "Closer, Pillie, hold me closer."

And he said, "If I hold you any closer, I'll be behind you." Just as he had when we were young: the line from Groucho Marx.

He hugged me for a long time, rocking me slightly back and forth. His kindness made me cry harder, and then I finally cried myself out.

William said, "Okay now, Lucy." He brushed back the thin strands of hair by my face. "I have a few suggestions."

"What," I said, and I ran the back of my hand against my nose.

"I think you should give up the apartment."

"I can't!" I kind of yelled this.

But William stayed calm, and he said, "All I am saying is just think about it. Okay? You don't have to do anything you don't want to. But just think about it. Are you listening to me?"

I nodded.

"Okay." He reached again and tucked my hair behind my ear, and he looked at me in a way that was very sweet and intimate. "Oh Button. You don't have to worry as much as you do."

"Why not?" I asked.

"Because you have me." He put his hand on the back of my head and gently pulled me toward him.

Afterward, I put my nightgown back on right away; I felt like a shy new bride.

William said to me, "So this is it, right?"

And I said, "You mean until we die?"

And he half-smiled, we were lying next to each other in his bed, and he reached to touch my nose with the tip of his finger and he said, "No, stupid-head, I mean forever and beyond."

We slept in the same bed every night after that, except sometimes he snored and I would go back to my own bed, but when he got up and felt anxious—I could half feel this in my sleep—I got up and went back into bed with him.

And that was that.

I will say this, and then I will not say any more about it:

But many, many years ago I knew a woman who had

had an affair with a man for six years, and he was impotent. I asked her—I knew her well at that time—what it was like to have an affair with a man who was impotent; he had had kidney surgery, I think, and it had left him this way. And this woman said to me—she was a quiet-spoken woman, and she said this to me with a small smile, she said this quietly—"Lucy, you would be surprised how little difference it makes."

And I thought: She was absolutely right. She was wrong, but she was also absolutely right.

~

But that first morning after, when I woke, William was gone! It turned out he had gone for his morning walk, but the fact that he had left me there alone in the bed, in the house, made me frightened.

"What's the matter?" he asked as he came through the door.

"Where did you *go*?" I said.

"For my walk. Sheesh, Lucy."

So there was that too. He was still William. And I was still me.

But we were also really happy then. We were.

~

One morning I said to William, "Shall we tell the girls?"

And he said, "You mean about us?"

"Yeah."

William sat down on the couch and squinted out the window. "I don't see why not." He hesitated and then said, "But it feels very private."

"That's exactly what I was thinking." I went and sat next to him.

He put his hand over mine. "We can tell them later." He glanced over at me. "We have the rest of our lives to let them know."

"I get it," I said.

vi

And then David came to me in a dream. He looked sick and gray and skinny and his eyes were sunken with a darkness around them, and he grabbed hold of me and was trying to pull me down into what looked like a big trash can that he was standing in, deep in the ground; I mean we really tussled. "No, David," I said. "No, I am not coming!" And I did not, and he disappeared into the great big trash can that was deep in the ground. But he was angry that I did not come with him.

In the morning I told William about the dream, and I said, "That was a fear dream, it wasn't really David."

Although I was not sure—at all—that it was not really David.

William said nothing.

～

I had a memory one night: Years ago, when William and I were living with our young girls in our apartment in New York City, I saw his shoes next to the bed. I had walked into the bedroom to hang up a shirt in his closet and there were his shoes, not his work shoes but his casual shoes, they were like docksiders—I think that is what they are called—leather with a leather string that went around them. And this is what I remembered: I was put off by them, the way their shape so clearly fit the feet of my husband, how the right one went slightly to the side. I was put off by them, by my husband's shoes.

Oh, the poor man!

And I thought: I wonder if he was ever put off by anything like that with me? He must have been.

These days his shoes did not put me off. I was always glad to see them on the porch.

~

I saw Charlene Bibber again one day. She was walking through the park in the middle of town and I went over to her and I said, "Charlene, hi!"

And she said, "Hi, Lucy."

So we spoke for a few minutes, she was still working at the food pantry and also at her job as a cleaner at the Maple Tree Apartments, and after a few minutes we sat on the ends of one of the benches there. We were both wearing our masks, although Charlene's mask was below her nose, and I asked how her summer was going, and she said, looking straight ahead, "Eh—"

"Well, why don't you walk with me?" I said.

So we agreed to take a walk by the river on Friday, which was her day off from work.

That Friday, Charlene was in the parking lot already when I got there, and we walked for a little and then she said, "Mind if we sit down on that bench? I'm on my feet all day cleaning and I'd like to sit."

"Oh, of course!" I said, so we sat down on a long granite slab of a bench; we were not six feet apart, but her mask was over her nose. And as we sat there she told me about the Maple Tree Apartments, she mentioned again Ethel MacPherson, whose one shoe she had stolen, and how bad she felt when the woman died.

I said I understood.

I told Charlene I thought my mind was going, and she said, "In what way?" And I said, Well, I couldn't remember things and I got confused a lot.

Charlene leaned her head a bit toward mine as though really listening, and then she nodded and said, "I feel that way too."

"You do?"

"Yeah, I do. And because I live by myself and can't really see anyone much, I get even more worried."

So we talked about that, about losing our minds, and then she told me about this woman she cleaned for, Olive Kitteridge, at the Maple Tree Apartments. "I feel really bad for her," Charlene said. "She has a friend, Isabelle, but Isabelle had to go over the bridge and now Olive seems depressed."

"What do you mean, over the bridge?" I asked, and Charlene explained that it was the next level of care after the independent part of living there, and it was more like a nursing home and you had to go literally over a little bridge to get there. So it was called "going over the bridge."

"Why did Isabelle have to go over the bridge?" I asked.

And Charlene said it was because Isabelle had fallen

and broken her leg and when she got out of rehab she couldn't live alone again. "It's so sad," Charlene said.

We sat in silence for a bit, and then Charlene said, "But Olive goes to see her every day. They say that Olive goes into her room and reads her the newspaper every day from front to back."

"Oh man," I said.

And Charlene said, "I know."

We agreed to meet again two Fridays from now.

vii

A week or so later—how do you know the time in a pandemic—but at some point after this, William, when I came back from my afternoon walk, was lying on the couch, and he said to me, "Lucy, I'm dizzy. I've been lying here for an hour waiting for you to come back and I am really dizzy."

"Why didn't you call me?" I said, sitting on the couch by his feet.

"I don't know." He said again, "But I'm really dizzy."

"Drink some water," I said, but I saw that he had a glass near him, and he reached and finished it, and I was scared. I called Bob Burgess. And Bob said he would call his doctor on his cellphone, it was okay, he and his doctor were friends.

Within five minutes Bob called back and said that the doctor had said to drink a liter of water and that the doctor would call him in ten minutes. So I made William drink four more glasses of water, and slowly he stopped being dizzy. But it was as though I had become stuck inside a block of wood, that is the only way to describe it. I sat there and we waited. William finally sat up. He looked old to me. And he didn't look at me, he just kept looking around the room. We waited more and William said he was far less dizzy, but then he lay down again and he fell asleep. I could not think, or feel, or anything, while we waited. An hour later William's phone rang and it was Bob's doctor, and after he talked to William for a while he said it was dehydration, that it was hot out, and people had to be careful.

So that happened. And then I made us scrambled eggs for supper and William seemed cheerful. But I was not cheerful.

The rest of the evening I felt quietly awful.

But after we went to bed that night and William had gone to sleep, I had a sudden memory: When I was very young they had shown us some movie in school. I have no memory at all what the movie was about, but I remember the anxiety of the teacher as she had to get the projector to work, and it did work, and this is all that I remember:

At the very beginning of the movie was a blue screen with many white ping-pong balls bouncing around on it, and every so often a ping-pong ball would bounce into another ping-pong ball and then bounce off again. This went on, the ping-pong balls bouncing around randomly and randomly hitting into one another. And in my memory I thought—even back then, so young—I thought: That is like people.

My point is, if we are lucky we bounce into someone. But we always bounce away again, at least a little.

And I thought of this that night, how my ping-pong ball had bumped into William's, and yet always—a little bit even now—bounced away, and I thought of David, whose ping-pong ball had really gone away from me now, and I thought of how Bob Burgess was right now with Margaret, who did not know that he needed a smoke on occasion; he was alone in that need. Except for when his ping-pong ball briefly bumped into mine and I knew about his need for a cigarette. And our ping-pong balls had bumped into each other when he called the doctor for us. And when we were together.

I thought of Charlene Bibber living alone, afraid she would lose her mind, and my ping-pong ball touching hers just briefly.

I had a sense then of being old, and William is even older; I thought how our time was almost done, and I had a real fear that William would die before me and I would be really lost.

In the middle of the night, William suddenly snorted after a snore, and he woke up, and he said "Lucy?" And I said "What?" And he said "Are you there?" And I said "I'm right here." And he went back to sleep immediately; I could tell by his breathing.

But I did not go back to sleep. I stayed awake and I thought: We all live with people—and places—and things—that we have given great weight to. But we are weightless, in the end.

~

A few weeks later I found out that William did not like watching me floss my teeth. He did not say this, but slowly it came to me that every night—or many nights—when we were talking in the living room I might floss my teeth and a certain look went over his face, I mean he became extra closed down, and I suddenly said, "William! Do you hate to see me floss my teeth?"

And he said, "Kind of."

"Why haven't you told me?" I asked.

And he just shrugged.

I felt really embarrassed. And part of this was remembering how I had not liked seeing his shoes when we were young and married.

~

One night during this time Margaret and Bob and William and I went down to the marina for dinner. They did not let people inside the restaurant, there was only one section of the porch that was open, but it was a very popular place, a lot of people from New York and Connecticut and Massachusetts were there. You could see by their license plates, and also I could tell from just seeing the people themselves, how they were dressed, differently from the locals, and I was surprised the whole summer by this, how people continued to come to Maine in the middle of a pandemic. Even while I, myself, had done the same thing.

But the point is this:

They had picnic tables nearby, and this is where the four of us sat. William went to the front door to pick up the food we had ordered earlier by phone, and this is where we had sat with Katherine Caskey that night, only tonight we were closer to the porch area of the actual restaurant, and this is what I saw:

A really well-dressed woman, I mean she was wearing black jeans and a blue shirt and her hair was really well done, blond but not brassy—this woman, who was maybe fifty at the most, sat with a man, I could not see him as well, but he seemed her counterpart—and this couple sat there, and I watched them, and they did not speak once during the entire meal. The woman's face was a pretty-enough face, but it was a sad face, and as I watched she had four white wines, one after the other. They brought the wine in a plastic cup, I think because of the pandemic, and that woman sat there, and I watched her drink four cups of white wine while her husband—or whoever he was—never spoke to her, nor she to him.

I have finally seen enough of the world to know that they were well-off, or certainly much better off than the people who came from this town, and yet there they were. And I am only telling you that I understood—which of course I have understood before—that money makes no difference in these kinds of things.

You may say: Well, she was an alcoholic. But I saw her differently, even if she was an alcoholic.

· · ·

I felt that I had seen a private terror I was not supposed to have seen. And so I did not speak of it to anyone, not to William or even to Bob. But I will never forget that woman's face. Her sadness. Her pain. Her fear. It's funny the things we remember, even when we think we are not remembering well anymore.

Five

i

"I am in mourning for my life," William said to me cheerfully after breakfast one day a few weeks later as we sat on the couch and watched a summer rain come down.

"That's a line from Chekhov," I said. "How do you know that? I'm surprised you know that. It's from *The Seagull*."

He shrugged. "Estelle and her endless auditions." And then William repeated, "I am in mourning for my life."

It took me a moment. We were sitting on the couch facing the water, watching the rain pelting down. "You really are?" I said. I turned to look at him.

"Of course I am." His hair had grown in abundantly, and with his mustache back—but it was not all the way back, and his scalp had spots of baldness on it—he looked both familiar to me and yet a version of a man much older than I thought of William. I thought he must mean because of his prostate that he had said that. But I just said, "Tell me."

"Oh Lucy, come on. I sit here and think over my life, and I think, Who have I been? I have been an idiot."

"In what way?" I asked him.

And interestingly he answered first about his profession. "I have taught student after student after student, but did I make a real contribution to science? No."

I opened my mouth, but he held up his hand to stop me.

"And on a personal level, look how I have lived my life."

I thought he must have been talking about his affairs. But he was not. He said, pointing out the window, "Look at that tower, Lucy. My father's father—that horrible old man we met when we went to Germany so many years ago—my *grandfather* was making money on World War II." He looked over at me. "He was making money on these submarines that were coming right into this harbor. He was a huge industrialist, and all he cared about was making money, and he did—during the war. And he stuck it all in Switzerland." He hesitated for a long time, looking out the window.

Then he looked at me again. "And I took that money, Lucy. Don't tell me how much I've given away, I know I've given away a lot of money, but no one ever gives away enough to actually change their lifestyle, and so I took that money, and I still have that money." He looked away, then back at me. "And it makes me absolutely sick."

. . .

I said nothing. Out of respect, I stayed quiet.

William stood up and said softly, "Even my mother told me I shouldn't take the money, but I did." He walked to the window and looked out, and then he turned back to me and said, "Did you know that my father—right before he died—he was supposed to come into that money, and *he didn't take it*."

I was really surprised to hear that, and I said so.

William sighed, and sat down again on the couch, and said, "That's why my mother didn't think I should take it, because my father was decent enough not to. And I rationalized it for years. It was mine, I told myself, no different from any rich kid who gets money from his CEO father. But it *is* different. My grandfather made it on a war that was unbelievably horrifying. My father didn't want it, and I did."

William stood up again, and he kept walking around as he spoke. He said, "My grandfather was greedy and he was smart. And what's happening in this country right now is mostly because of greed as well." He turned back to face me. He said, "And you can say, Well, just give it away, William, what's the big deal? But if I gave it all away today, and I'm not going to, what difference would it make? None. But it's money that was the result of huge damage in this world, and the world can be damaged all over again. And I have just lived here with that money all these years." He turned and sat back down on the couch and pushed his hand through his hair, which made his hair stand up in different ways.

I waited quite a while to see if he had anything more to say, but he seemed not to. Finally I said, "Well, you know, William. I've always had a theory about people who have losses and then think they are owed something." I gave him examples: of people who had lost a child and then embezzled from the church they had been a secretary at for years, or people who shoplifted after finding out their husband was going to die. . . . And then I said, "You lost your father when you were fourteen, William. And so I think you thought you were owed." I added, "I mean, I think it's just human."

William answered, with no affect to his voice, that he was fourteen when his father died and he was in his midthirties when the money came to him through the trust he had never known was there, and I said, "That doesn't matter."

But I could tell he was not listening, he was not going to be convinced.

. . .

But this is what had been eating away at William. That he had taken money from that man—his horrible grandfather with his glittering eyes—and that William had increasingly hated himself for doing this, more so as he saw the state of the world unfolding. I saw that it must have made him feel aligned with his grandfather and at odds with his father, who had not taken the money.

And it seemed that my ping-pong ball could not touch his right now. We are alone in these things that we suffer.

But then William's face brightened considerably and he said to me, "So my plan is this: I am going to give a ton of it to the University of Maine at Presque Isle and really help develop a place to get those potato parasites studied. Because it's not just parasites, Lucy." And he went on to tell me how climate change had made the season longer for potatoes, but that was not a good thing, they had more pests as a result, and they were trying to develop a new kind of potato. He sat back and nodded. "*That's* what I'm going to do," he said.

ii

One warm afternoon in August, Bob Burgess showed up, and I had the sense later that William was expecting him.

"Here he is," William said, or something like that, and he went out to meet him on the lawn. When I came out of the house Bob gave me a big wave and said to William, "Ready?" And William said, "Let's do it."

So Bob got back into his car, and William opened the passenger-side door of our car for me, and I said, "What are you doing?" And he just said, "Let's see."

We followed Bob back to town. It was a glorious day, the water was beautiful as we drove over the small bridge, on both sides the water seemed green and sweetly friendly to me; it still had the white waves that hit the rocks all the time. As we got into town we followed Bob's car down Main Street, and then Bob pulled into a parking spot near the shops—there is a bookstore (which was only doing pickup), and a furnishings store that was closed, and a tea shop that was open and sold a variety of things—and we pulled in next to him. Then we followed Bob around to the back of the building that the bookstore was in—there was a parking lot filled with potholes, and you could see the fire station from there—and Bob brought out a key and opened a door: You would not even have noticed the door if you didn't know it was there, I mean it was just a plain steel painted pale green thing—and inside was a steep wooden staircase, and we followed him single file up the staircase, and then at the top of the staircase was a door off to the right, and Bob found a different key, and we walked through that door into a little tiny hallway and there was *another* door to the right, and Bob unlocked that and stood back and held his hand out toward the doorway.

Bob said, "Here you go, Lucy. Your own studio."

I did not understand what was happening at first. But in the room, and it was not a small room, were a table and a big upholstered chair, and a couch and also two bookcases and two lamps on small tables. "What is this?" I asked.

And William said, "We found a studio for you, Lucy." His face was filled with emotion, he was really worked up. He said, "For you to work in."

And they stood there, those two men, with such looks of suppressed excitement on both of their faces—

I could not believe it.

I have never had a room to work in. Of my own. Never.

iii

My apartment in New York bothered me more and more, and each time I thought about it, I thought: No. That is what I thought. One night—it was toward the end of August and I had spent the day at my studio—when I came home I told William again, as I had that night of my panic attack, about how I felt about my apartment in New York, and I could see that he was hearing me. He asked me when the lease got renewed.

I said, "The end of September."

He leaned forward, his arms on his knees. "Then give it up, Lucy."

And I said, "I can't give it up!"

And he sat back and said, "Why not?"

"Because I can't go to New York with this virus—how could I move anything out?"

William sat with his arms on the chair arms and said, "Bob will get some guys here from town and they'll go get what you want. It's a tiny place, Lucy. Think about what's in it that you want, and Bob will have some guys bring it up here. For now. We can figure the rest out later."

I sat and said nothing as I absorbed this.

William added, "And now is the time to do it, because New York is not in terrible shape at the moment, but there will be another surge when it gets cold. So let's do this now."

"Really?" I asked.

He just raised his eyebrows at me.

And so by the middle of September, with help from Bob— who found three young men ready and excited about doing

the job, they had never been to New York City—my things
were moved up to Maine from New York. I gave everything in the kitchen to Marie, who helped me with my
cleaning: She FaceTimed me from my apartment. And I
gave her most of my clothes as well. I also gave her most
of the linens and most of the towels. Her aunt wanted the
bed, and they had it moved to her aunt's place in the
Bronx. My building manager—a young woman—was extremely good about all this; usually someone has to be
there if you are moving out, and certain insurance things
have to be filled out by the movers, but the manager let the
guys come in and take the things that were left; she was
very nice about it, as I have said. I told Marie I would give
her a year's severance pay; she—or, rather, her husband,
the doorman—had come into the apartment every week
to water my plant; it was—along with David's cello—the
only thing in the apartment I really cared about.

When I saw the plant, almost eight feet tall, standing so
shyly on our porch, I couldn't believe it. I could not believe
I had done this. I put David's cello in the spare bedroom
upstairs, the one with the bookcase in it and the trees
pressing up against the windows.

When I thought of the New York apartment, I thought: It
is gone, as all things will be gone someday.

iv

From New York had come four large cardboard boxes filled with old writings and photos of mine, and so one day William helped me take those to my studio, and I went through the boxes slowly. It was very strange. There were photos of me in college, with William, and with other friends. I looked so young and happy!

I found a journal entry from back when I had been living with William and the girls—they were about eight and nine at the time—and I had decided to have someone come in and clean the apartment. It was a young man who had arrived; he was very sweaty and anxious-looking, and I recorded in my journal how I felt sorry for him while he vacuumed with sweat dripping off his nose. But then this young man had gone into the bathroom for quite a while, and after he left I went into the bathroom and I realized that he had masturbated in there, and I had a very bad reaction to this.

I had forgotten the incident until I read it there in my young handwriting. Of course I had been frightened by this, because my father would so frequently do the same thing during my childhood. According to the journal entry, William did not care when I told him. I mean he sort of shrugged it off.

I had called the young man and told him we did not need him anymore.

It was a strange thing to go through those papers.

I found this: a birthday card from my mother. As soon as I saw it I remembered: It was the last card she ever sent me, the year before she died. On the front were pretty violet-colored flowers. When I opened it up, the card had printed on it: Happy Birthday. And below it was simply—

    M.

V

William and I continued to take car trips. We did not feel safe spending the night anywhere else, but we would drive to various places and then come back home. In late September, William and I drove to a town called Dixon; it was almost two hours away. The town was built along a river, and there was a paper mill that had once employed thousands, but it had mostly closed down many years earlier;

only one hundred people still worked there. William was interested in the old mills; he had researched this one and said that the man who had started the mill in the late 1800s was from England and that he had made houses for the millworkers that were quite beautiful; it was called Bradford Place. William had shown me a photograph of the houses online, and they did seem lovely, built on the hills throughout the town, two-family places of brick, with wide porches. On top of the hill was a huge cathedral. The photograph was from the 1950s.

What we found was appalling.

The town was like a ghost town, but when William drove up to where the houses had been built for the millworkers, we saw a few people out in front of them. The houses were in terrible shape; they seemed to spew forth their guts onto their front lawns. Broken bicycles and large black bags of garbage and a broken windowframe, these things were in front of the houses; some of the porches were piled with what looked to be junk.

Some of the houses had huge American flags draped over their front windows or on their porches. The few people who were outside stood and watched us as we drove by.

"Oh God," William said.

. . .

We went back into the center of town, and William got out to go into a gas station store to buy two bottles of water. I stayed in the car, and I saw that there was a policeman in his cruiser right beside me; he wore no mask, and he kept looking at his phone, and every so often he would pick up a big paper cup and drink through the straw in it.

I watched him so carefully.

So carefully I watched him.

I wondered, What is it like to be a policeman, especially now, these days? What is it like to be *you*?

I need to say: This is the question that has made me a writer; always that deep desire to know what it feels like to be a different person. And I could not stop feeling a fascination for this man, who seemed to be in his fifties, with a decent face and strong-looking arms. In a way that is not uncommon for me as a writer, I sort of began to feel what it was like to be inside his skin. It sounds very strange, but it is almost as though I could feel my molecules go into him and his come into me.

And then three young guys came out of the gas station store, and they stood in the parking lot opening bags of potato chips and laughing, but they scared me in a way;

they all had very pasty skin and their eyes said that they had nothing left in this world to lose. The youngest one was probably thirteen and he looked especially sad; his teeth were skinny and sort of bucked, and you could tell that he was trying to impress the two older ones, and they were not impressed.

William got back into the car and we drove around more; we saw the mill that, according to William, had sent its paper all over the world back in the day, to Europe, even to South Africa. As we drove along the river, I saw down on the embankment—through the trees—a few broken-down old cottages.

As we headed back to Crosby, I said, "I was watching a policeman who was sitting in his cruiser while you were in the store. I'm going to write a story about him."

William glanced over at me.

"His name is going to be Arms Emory. And he has a brother named Legs in the next town who sells insurance. They're called Arms and Legs because they used to play football when they were kids, they were the stars. Arms could throw that football like the wind, and Legs could run down the field like a crazy man."

"Okay," William said.

.   .   .

Back in my studio I started the story. I loved Arms. He would be a supporter of our current president; this seemed true to me. Then I realized that his brother, Legs, would have fallen off a ladder six years earlier when he was cleaning the gutters, and as a result he got hooked on pain-killers.

I called Margaret, who put me in touch with a social worker who counseled drug users, and I spoke with this drug counselor for a long time so that I would understand Legs's situation. Then Margaret had me call a man who had once been on the police force, and he was enormously helpful as well. He said, "Cops take care of each other."

I thought about the story. Then I began to write.

Arms Emory's father had worked in the mill back when it was fully operative; he had worked in the pulping room. They had lived in one of the beautiful houses in Bradford Place that William and I had seen. Back then, the houses were still beautiful. When the boys were young, their father died, and their mother—whom Arms thought of as practically a saint—moved them to a new house, and she got a job at the hospital, and she told her sons that what they did reflected on their father, so even now Arms did not drink. His happiest days had been on the football field in high school when he and his brother were the football stars. Arms loved his brother deeply.

I sat in the overstuffed chair in my studio and thought about these two men. Once in a while I would write a scene, but mostly I just sat, staring at nothing. Just thinking about them.

I realized that the youngest kid I had seen in the gas station store parking lot, his name would be Sperm Peasley. He would be called Sperm as a joke—because he was so pale and small that it looked like his parents had conceived him with two sheets between them. But he never thought of his name anymore. The older of the two fellows with him would be called Jimmie Wagg. He would be the drug dealer of the town. And the middle kid was Sperm's cousin. They had just stolen the potato chips from the store, I decided. And Sperm was still young enough to get a real kick out of that.

I wrote these sentences: "But there was an exhaustion Arms felt these days; it left him too tired to fight with his wife—he had not liked her for a number of years—and it left him too tired to think of the election. And yet there was an anxiety he felt as well. He did not see the connection between his anxiety and his fatigue; he was not a reflective man."

. . .

I wrote about how, right before the pandemic, Arms had attended a meeting with other cops about police reform. And how glad he had been to see these others; he was respected, he was a sergeant. He had led them through the routine: no chokeholds, no excessive force.

I would put the story aside and sit in the overstuffed chair and think about it. But writing it— I had not been that happy for quite a while. I was able to work.

vi

One night at dinner I spoke to William of my brother and how sad I felt his life was, and William said, "Lucy, I don't want to hear this. You've told me this before, and I don't want to hear it again."

"Fine," I said.

But here is the other memory I had of my brother when I mentioned much earlier that I remembered him being beaten up on the playground:

The memory is this:

I was young, my brother was older, he may have been

seven at the time. When I walked into the house one day, my brother was lying on the living room floor and he was whimpering, and I saw—my mother took in sewing and alterations to make money—I saw that my brother had a series of straight pins stuck into his forearm. I could not believe it. My mother was on the floor leaning over him. I screamed, and what I always remember is that my mother looked up at me and said with an odd smile, "Do you want some too?"

And I ran out of the house.

One of the reasons I believe this memory to be true is, first of all, it was so strange.

And also because I remember going with my mother and my brother to the local doctor's office some time later than this; my brother required a shot, and when he saw the doctor bring out the syringe, my brother ran like an animal, he could not get away from the man fast enough; I remember he ended up crawling underneath the doctor's desk, and he was crying. And I remember the doctor looking at my mother. And my mother laughed and said something like: What can you do?

I had told William about this when we were first married and he had not said anything. But when I started to see a psychiatrist, my lovely woman psychiatrist, she had nodded slightly and said quietly, "Oh Lucy." What I mean is I think she believed me.

William said that night, waving a hand, "There's nothing new about it. I don't want to hear about your brother. Besides," he said, "he has that old couple that he went to the food bank with, or whatever."

"They're dead," I said. "The Guptills died a few years ago, and there is no place my brother can go with this pandemic." And William still did not want to hear about my brother's life.

But my brother's life had been, and still was, one of great solitariness. And he would arrive in my mind sometimes, as he did this night. I remembered that years ago my mother had told me—Pete would have been a grown man at that point—that my brother would spend the night in the Pedersons' barn—this was a barn that was closest to us—to be with the pigs that were going to be taken to slaughter the next day.

And then William began to talk about his "nephews and nieces"—the children of Lois Bubar's children, and the children of Dave and his brothers, and how well they had all done, and he went on and on—I had heard this before, so often—about how they were so smart, and they read books! He said this to me that night, after not wanting to hear about my brother, and I remembered: William does not like to hear anything negative.

Many people do not. William is not alone in that.

~

By the middle of October the foliage was beautiful. It seemed that the colors had arrived somewhat late, and because there had been so little rain for so long people thought maybe this was why the trees were shy and would not change their color so vibrantly. But then they did! Then they did.

Here is a secret about the beauty of the physical world:

My mother told me this when I was very small—my real mother, not the nice mother I made up later to be with me—my real mother told me one day that the great landscape painters understood one thing: that everything in nature started from the same color. And I thought of this as I watched the leaves changing. You may think: Don't be ridiculous! There are vibrant reds and yellows and greens! And there are. Yet, walking along the river, as I did more frequently now, but also walking down our narrow road, I saw this. That in the yellows and the reds and the greens, they were somehow springing from the same color, and it is hard to describe this, but as more leaves fell I saw this more clearly. Everything seems to start with a kind of brown and it grows from there: The huge slabs of rocks that were on the side of the road were gray and brown, and the oak trees that had turned russet were similar in color to the seaweed that I have described as being a coppery color, and the water, whether it is dark green or gray or brown, was of a similar hue.

I also noticed how, in the afternoons, clouds might start to come in and they were gently autumnal; they made the world look quietly soft as though it was already getting ready to tuck itself in for the night.

I am only saying: What a thing the physical world is!

vii

William took another trip to Sturbridge to see Bridget and Estelle. When he returned this time, he did not weep. He said that Bridget had made two friends in Larchmont— one a girl next door, and also that girl's friend, and Bridget seemed much happier. "Of course, she's such a great kid," he said. But! Estelle's boyfriend had dumped her. Or Estelle had dumped him. "Are you ready for this?" He looked at me ruefully. "The guy was gay."

"He was *gay*?" I said. "And she didn't know that?"

"Guess not." William sat on the couch with his arms spread out across the top of it. "He was older, I didn't know that part. And I guess he was of the generation where some men didn't want to be gay."

"Oh William, that's so sad," I said. I added, "For all of them."

"Not sad for Bridget."

"But does Estelle seem okay?"

"Seems to be. She was cheerful as she told me this. Who knows? She's Estelle. She'll be fine."

"Yeah, well, still—" I said.

"Oh, I know, I know." But he began to whistle, which I had not heard him do in years.

~

"Hey, Lucy, do you want to buy this place?" William asked me this the next morning. We still had the screens on the big porch and we ate our breakfast out there, though it was chilly. I had wanted to put the plexiglass back up, but every time I mentioned it William said, "Not yet, Lucy."

"Buy this place? You're kidding." I was almost standing

up, but I sat down again; we had just finished breakfast. There was a steady rain falling outside and the water was swirling like mad.

"Not really. Bob just offered me a very good price on it."

So I sat and looked at this man I had been married to, with whom I had two daughters, and with whom I was, so many years later, now sharing a bed again. Finally I said, "Is it already predetermined?"

And he laughed in a way and took my hand and said, "No, Lucy." Then he looked at me and said, "Probably." He shrugged. "Whatever."

I said, "We'll die in this house if we buy it."

And William said, "Well, we have to die someplace." And I said, "That's true."

He got up and went inside and I followed him. He walked slightly stooped; he was no longer a young man; he was no longer even a middle-aged man. Sitting down on the couch he said, patting his thigh, "Come here, Lucy. Sit on my lap. I love it when you sit on my lap."

I sat on his lap and he said, "Now listen. We need to become residents of Maine. There's going to be a vaccine, maybe even by the end of the year, and we're sure not going back to New York to get it. We'll have to get it here."

I pulled back to look at him. "Seriously?" I said.

"Seriously."

We sat quietly for many moments, and then I said, "Let's buy the house."

William said, "I already did."

~

So we became residents of Maine. I could not believe it, but we did. William had no trouble with this, his sister lived here, his nephews and nieces, and he had his whole new career. But I called my accountant, my dear accountant—he had left the city, given up his office, and moved upstate—and he said, Yes, he could still do my taxes, but he said, "Lucy, if you do this, you have to mean it. You can't move back to New York next year. You have to spend more than half the year in Maine," and I said: Okay. There was a sense of unreality to it for me.

We went and got Maine driver's licenses, and I worried that when the man who sat behind the counter saw that I was from New York he might say something. But he said nothing, and took two pictures of me, because he thought the first one was not good.

~

I called Estelle one day not long after that. "Oh Lucy!" she said. "How nice to hear your voice!" I told her we had become residents of Maine, and she said she thought that was probably the best thing to do. "But it's strange," I said to her, and she said, "Oh, it must be!" Then she said how it hadn't worked out with her partner—this is what she called him—and I said I was sorry about that, and she said, "Well, I knew he was bisexual, I just didn't know that he wouldn't want to give up men once he was with me." I did not quite know what to say to that, and Estelle said, "But it's okay." She laughed her burbling laughter and she said, "Oh Lucy, don't you sometimes just feel sorry for everyone in this whole wide world?" And I understood then why William had fallen in love with her. "I know exactly what you mean," I said. We talked more, and she was very cheerful. "Bye-bye!" she said, right before we hung up.

~

I still felt that my mind was odd. I still would not remember what it was that I had been about to say. I still walked into a room and wondered why I had come into the room. It worried me, though Bob kept telling me he was the same way.

· · ·

And Charlene Bibber said she kept feeling the same way. We still walked together—or mostly sat on the granite slab— every other week, and one time she said to me, "I'm glad we don't talk politics." I turned to look at her. "We never have to talk politics," I said, and she said she knew that. "I just appreciate it," she said. And I said, "Of course."

The river walk was beautiful now, so many oranges and yellows, and that day there were many yellow leaves on the ground because it had been windy the night before, it was like a carpet of yellow we walked on. And the sun streamed down on it.

We sat on one of the granite slab benches, and Charlene told me she was glad she had the job cleaning at the Maple Tree Retirement Home.

She told me again about Olive Kitteridge. "She's very liberal, she talks about the president all the time, she just hates him. But it's okay, because she's nice to me. Well, not *nice,* Olive isn't exactly nice to anyone, but I can tell she likes me, and she's really lonely. Sometimes I just sit and we talk for a long time. She loves birds. And she talks about her first husband, Henry, that's her favorite subject, and I talk about my husband."

"That's nice," I said.

Charlene put her hand on her chin.

"It is," she said.

When we parted she said, "Lucy, you've got to tell me if you think I'm losing my mind."

"All right," I said. "You have to tell me the same thing."

And we waved goodbye.

As I drove home from the river that day, this thought arrived: There was a faint odor of loneliness that came from Charlene. And the awful truth is this: It had made me draw back just slightly inside myself. And I knew this was because I had always been afraid of giving off that odor myself.

~

William was really excited about the potato parasites. He was on the phone a great deal with Dave and other members of Lois's family, and he was also on the phone with Lois herself—they were planning one more get-together in Orono before the weather got too cold, and Dave was going to come with her. The climate change issue was becoming more interesting to William, and he was trying to help them develop a new kind of potato, one that could survive wet and warmth. He spoke about all this to me, and the people he had come to know, and I found myself getting interested. I thought how when a person is really excited about something, it can be contagious.

I first noticed this years ago when I was very young and taught at that community college in Manhattan. I was so enthusiastic about the books I had read that I could see my students watching me and getting interested in these books too—just because I was so excited about these books that I had recently read.

viii

Toward the end of October it was supposed to rain straight through one weekend, and I noticed, but only vaguely, that William seemed to be checking the weather a lot, and he seemed disturbed by the rain that was supposed to come. I had asked him again if we could please put the plexiglass back up on the porch—we were no longer eating out there, it was too cold, although the porch had a heater—and he again said, "We'll do it soon."

But on Friday it was not yet raining, and he said, "Come on, Lucy, let's drive to Freeport, to L.L.Bean. We don't have to go in, let's just drive there."

So we did. I was always willing to go anywhere, because there was so little to do.

I was surprised by all the people that were going in and out of the store. "Let's just sit here," William said. There were iron rod tables and chairs spread out at safe distances, and because the weather looked like it would rain at any minute they were empty. But we sat at one of the tables, there was a roof over it, and William said, "Perfect." He kept checking his phone.

"What are we doing here?" I asked. "I mean, I'm fine, I'm just surprised that—"

And then—*oh dear God!!*—our daughters were walking over to us, both of them waving their arms wildly. "Mom!" they called; they almost screamed it: "Mom!" And people turned to look at me. "Dad!" They yelled this and walked toward us, waving their arms over their heads, and I could not believe it.

I could not believe it.

Chrissy and Becka walked to the table—William and I were now standing up—and they put their arms out and made hugging motions; even with their masks on, I could see their happiness just beaming forth.

I have never seen anything as beautiful as those girls. These women. My daughters!

They were laughing and laughing—and William was beaming behind his mask as well, as he glanced at me. I said, "William! You planned this?"

"We all did," Chrissy said. "We wanted to surprise you, so we did."

They sat down at the table, and William and I sat down,

and we began to talk, oh, we talked and talked and talked. They had flown from New York to Boston and then rented a car and driven up from there. Becka said, "We didn't trust our driving skills to drive all the way from Connecticut," and I understood. Both girls had been raised in the city and had learned to drive late in their lives. They had reservations at the hotel in Crosby, William had helped arrange all of this. "We had to come now, before the numbers start going back up," Chrissy said. "So we did!"

"Oh my God," I kept saying, "Oh my God."

Then I said, "Becka, why do you look so tall?" And she said, "Oh, it must be my sneakers, you haven't seen these," and she stuck her foot forward to me and I saw that the sole of her red sneaker was very thick.

She had bought them online. Then Becka said, "Mom, I have to tell you about these pajamas I ordered online. They came from a really reputable place, and made in the U.S." But, she told me, when they arrived they looked like what people in concentration camps had to wear; they were really wide-striped, and every time she put them on, or even when they were just lying over a chair, she could not get it out of her head how they looked like concentration camp uniforms, and so she had written the place and told them, and they couldn't have been nicer, and they even took them off their website, and then they sent her a different pair of pajamas, solid dark blue.

Sitting there, the four of us: Chrissy speaking to her father, me speaking to Becka, then we would all speak together. There had been almost no one on the plane. They had ordered a truck at the rental place—this made Chrissy bend over in her chair laughing—but when they went to pick it up they decided to take a real car instead. They pointed their hands in the direction where the car was, but it was too far away to see.

Finally they went and got into their car and followed us to Crosby and we drove to the one hotel in town, where they checked in. The hotel lobby was big and empty, and so we sat in different corners of it and kept on talking. Always with our masks on. Chrissy said, "Mom, this town is so cute." And Becka said, "It *really* is."

Then we drove ahead of them to the house, and we had dinner on the porch—this is why William had objected to putting the plexiglass back up, because he knew the girls were coming—and we kept talking and talking and talking. They loved the house. I was astonished at how much they said they loved it. "Mom, this is *great*, it's so funky," Chrissy said, sticking her head inside the door—but she would not go in, she only stayed on the porch, where the windows were open. "You guys should paint the walls white, oh, that's a brilliant idea," she said, turning to us with her eyes shining.

"Oh *yeah*," Becka said, "paint all the walls white. And

also the mantel—just everything. Make it all white. What a place, you guys."

"Your father just bought it," I said.

"You *did*?" They said this at the same time, turning to look at William. Then Chrissy said, "Oh, what fun! It's really adorable."

I do think this: I do think it was the happiest I have been in my life.

Then Chrissy told us that she and Michael had bought the house in Connecticut from Michael's parents—she and Michael were not going to return to New York. "There's no need to," Chrissy said. "We've grown used to the place, so we're putting our apartment on the market."

I was surprised. "Why didn't you tell us?"

And she shrugged and said, "Well, I just did."

Becka was still in the guesthouse, but she was going to move to an apartment in New Haven. She was thinking about going back to school.

"What kind of school?" William asked, and she said she wasn't sure yet. And then she said, "Okay, okay, law school. I took the boards and did *really* well, you guys! I've applied to Yale."

"Jesus," William said.

"I know," Becka said. "Let's not talk about it anymore."

. . .

On Sunday afternoon, as they were getting into their car to leave, I said to them, "Dad and I got back together." And both of their faces looked stunned. "You did?" They asked this almost at the same time, one speaking over the other. William had already said goodbye, he was standing on the porch. "You *did*?" Chrissy was the one who repeated this, and I was sort of surprised at how surprised they were. Chrissy got into the car behind the wheel, and Becka said, "Mom, turn your face away," and she hugged me, we were both of course wearing our masks. William and I waved to them as they drove down the steep driveway.

I noticed that I did not feel sad. William said, "Let's take a ride," and so we did. We wended our way around the small roads along the coast, and I said, "They left an afterglow," and he looked at me and said, "Yeah, they did."

~

If I had known what it would be like the next time that I saw them— Well, I did not know then.

It is a gift in this life that we do not know what awaits us.

Six

i

And then it was November and the election took place. I feel no point to recording all of that. I will only say that it was a very tense time for me, and also for most of the country.

~

On Thanksgiving, William and I decided to have beans and hot dogs. For some reason we thought this was a wonderful idea. We had red kidney beans from a can and two hot dogs each, and I made an apple pie, and the day felt so cozy. I remember that day so clearly.

~

My brother had told me that he was going to Vicky's house for Thanksgiving; he did that every year. And I said to him, "But it won't be safe, Pete. She goes to church without a mask," and he said not to worry, he would wear a mask and it was just the kids, and their kids, who were going to be there. "But that's the problem," I said. "All those people." And then I stopped, because it came to me that for my brother, who spent day after day after day of his life alone, Thanksgiving had been special to him always, because of Vicky and her family. When we were kids we would go to the Congregational church and have their free Thanksgiving dinner, and even I remember that the people there were nice to us on that day. I understood why it was important for Pete to go, so I stopped. And we just chatted about whatever we chatted about, and that was that.

~

A week after Thanksgiving my sister had the virus. Her youngest daughter, Lila, called to tell me, and she was crying. "She's in the hospital and we can't even go see her. They're putting her on a ventilator." I listened, and I spoke to my niece quietly, but I could not console her. I asked if her mother could speak on the telephone and Lila said, "No," but the next day I received a text from my sister, and it said, Lucy this is not fun and I do not think I will make it.

I texted back immediately: I love you.

And later that night she answered: I know you think you do.

The next day she sent me a text: Lucy you've always thought you were better than me. And I think you have been very selfish in your life. I'm sorry but I do. I should pray for you but I am too tired.

I felt like she had shot me in the chest. This is what it felt like to me.

On the phone my brother sounded tired, and noncommittal. When I said, "She called me selfish," he said nothing. So I asked him, "Do you think I'm selfish?" And he said, "Well, no, Lucy."

Vicky did not die of the virus, but my brother did. He called me from his house and said he had chills—his teeth were chattering—and he had shortness of breath, and I begged him to go to the hospital, but he said, "I'll be okay."

"Oh, *please* go!" I said, and after a moment he said, "Okay, maybe tomorrow."

Before we hung up he said, "Hey, Lucy."

And I said, "What, Petie?"

He said, "I don't want you to think you were selfish. That's just Vicky talking."

"Oh Petie, thank you," I said.

And then he said quietly, "I love you, Lucy. Bye now."

My brother had never said he loved me. No one in our family ever said that.

When he didn't answer his phone the next day, I almost called Vicky's husband to ask him to go over there, but then I thought, No, I will call the police. And so I did, and a serious-sounding fellow said he would drive there and check on him, and I kept saying, Thank you, oh, thank you.

And half an hour later the police called and told me that my brother, Pete Barton, had been found dead. He had died on his bed, the same bed that my father had died on many years earlier.

~

The grief I had was terrible. At first it was terrible because I kept thinking how Vicky had called me selfish. This is what killed me. I kept murmuring out loud: I was just trying to save my life. I thought about my brother, how pale he had always been, I thought of the boys beating him up on the playground, of the pins my mother had stuck into his arm. He never had a chance, I kept murmuring that too.

When I spoke to Vicky, who was by now home from the hospital, she sounded calm, and I understood that this was because she thought my brother was in heaven. And I thought what a bad life my sister had also had. She had her children, and even her husband, but all I could do was to picture her as a child, how she had never smiled, how she was always alone at school. There was one image I had of her walking past the art room one day, she had been alone and she looked frightened, and it was an image that seared itself into me that day; she had seen me and looked away—we never spoke in school when we saw each other. I had almost not liked her that day, I mean I had felt put off by her, by her loneliness and her look of fear. Both of which I had felt myself for all those childhood years.

I remembered the last time I had seen my brother and Vicky—a few years ago now, but I had gone to visit my brother while I was on a book tour in Chicago. I had rented a car and driven two hours to that tiny awful childhood home that he still lived in, and while I was there Vicky had come over, and we got to talking—the three of us—about our childhood, our mother in particular. And then I had a terrible panic attack, and I asked Vicky if she would drive me back to Chicago, and I asked Pete to follow us in my rental car. And they had done that! My sister had put me in her car, and she had driven toward the city of Chicago, she had done that for me!

Before we got to Chicago my panic had gone down, so I was able to switch cars with Pete and take my own rental car back. I said goodbye to them on the side of a four-lane highway. That was the last time I saw my sister. And my brother.

But they had been willing to do that for me!

I understood exactly why Vicky had called me selfish.

William had to sit in front of me, holding both my hands that night, looking me in the eye and telling me I had come from a very, very sad family, and if I had stayed there my life would have been sad as well. "And look what you've done, Lucy," William said. "Look at all the people you have helped with your books."

I have always wanted my books to help people.

But in truth, I have no sense that they do. Even if someone writes to me and says, Your books have helped me—while I am always glad to get the note—I have never really been able to believe it. I mean, praise seems unable to enter me.

ii

One night there was a huge storm with high winds and we lost our power. I woke in the night because I was cold, and William was already up. "The power went out," he said, not unhappily.

I said, "What do we do?" And he said, "We wait."

"But I'm so cold," I said, and he went and got the other quilts from the other beds, but they were not enough to stop me from shivering.

As a child I had often not been able to sleep at night because I was so cold. I thought of that now—how there had been a few nights when I had called out to my mother because I was so cold, and she had brought me a hot water bottle! I could still remember the rubbery smell of it, it was red, and not very big, but it was so warm, and I wouldn't know where to put it on my body, because wherever I put it, the comfort I felt from it was just enormous, but it made the rest of my small body feel bereft, and so I would shift it around from place to place; all this I remembered that night we lost our power.

The next morning Bob Burgess brought us over three flashlights. "Keep one upstairs all the time, and keep the other two downstairs so you know where they are."

. . .

That same morning William drove me to my studio and then he went to L.L.Bean. When he picked me up later that afternoon he was quiet, but he reached over a few times and touched my hand as he drove. And when I went into our bedroom there were two down quilts, white as fluffy snow, looking so beautiful there on the bed.

At night William and I slept holding each other.

~

In December, I noticed a drop in my mood. It had to do with my brother's death; it was no longer Vicky calling me selfish, it was the single, horrifying fact of Pete's death. It felt to me as though my entire childhood had died. You might think—I would have thought—that I wanted every part of my childhood gone. But I did not want every part of my childhood gone. I wanted my brother alive, and he had died alone in that small house. I thought how he had not wanted to go to the hospital with the virus and I remembered how frightened he had been of getting that shot as a kid in the doctor's office, and I could not stop the sense of sadness; it was a sadness that went so deep it was like it was a physical illness.

And it got dark so early and it was so wintry and cold that I could not walk as much as I had when we first arrived in Maine. And there were no more social gatherings, it was too cold, and also Covid had come to Maine and was all over the state, and so we had to be very careful. I went most days to my studio over the little bookstore, and really, I might have gone mad without it. I still almost went mad. Everything seemed very difficult. To even clean the two bathrooms in the house seemed beyond me, though when I finally did clean them I noticed I felt better. For a few minutes. As is true with many people who feel poorly, there was a sense of shame that accompanied this. I did not want to tell William, and what was there to tell him anyway? There was nothing I could do but hold on.

But he knew, I think, and he tried to be good to me.

I was very grateful to have William, but grief is a solitary matter.

One night I lay awake in bed and I remembered this: After my father died, he came to me many times in dreams. He was checking on me, and then he would go away. But the last dream I had of him was this: He was in his red Chevy truck and he was driving it erratically; he looked sick, as he had been before he died. And in the dream I said to him, "It's okay, Daddy, I can drive the truck now."

Oh, the memory of this filled me with both happiness and sadness. I had loved him, my poor suffering very damaged father.

I can drive the truck now, I had said.

But as time went by I did not feel that I could drive the truck. I felt that I was only barely hanging on.

iii

On January sixth, as I came in from my afternoon walk to the cove, the television was on and William said, "Lucy, come here now and watch this." I sat down still wearing my coat and I saw people attacking the Capitol in Washington, D.C., and I watched this news as though it was the first days of the pandemic in New York, I mean that I kept looking at the floor and had the strange sense again that my mind—or body—was trying to move away. All I can remember of this now is watching a man smashing a window again and again, people pushing up against one another as they got into the building while the policemen tried to hold them back. Many different colors swam before me as I saw people climbing up walls, all moving together.

· · ·

I said to William, "I can't watch this," and I went upstairs
to the bedroom and closed the door.

And then I remembered this: When I was a child we went
to Thanksgiving at the Congregational church in our
town, as I have said, and I remember that the people who
served us the food were nice to us. And there was one
woman, her name was Mildred, she was tall and—to my
eyes—old, but she was very kind to me. And what I remembered now was hearing Mildred say to someone that
whenever she drove by the building where her husband
had died—years before—she turned her head and looked
away because she could not stand to look.

And my mother—my real mother, not the nice one I
made up years later—my mother was scathing about Mildred's looking away from that building where her husband
had died. My mother said she'd never heard of such foolishness in her life.

But now I thought of Mildred.

I thought about how I had practically thrown the computer back at William when he showed me Elsie Waters's
obituary. I thought about how I had looked at the floor so

often watching the news. I thought about how I had just walked out of the room while the Capitol was being ransacked.

I thought: Mildred, I am just like you. I look away too.

And I thought: We are only doing what we can to get through.

~

Over the next few weeks, William became intensely interested in the news. He said, "Lucy, there were Nazis there." And he told me—because I had not seen it—about the man wearing the Camp Auschwitz sweatshirt. He told me that there had been a swastika flag and that there were other shirts people wore with 6MWE on them, which were meant to indicate that six million Jews weren't enough to die.

I said, "But, William, someone had to know this was going to happen! I mean in the government, someone had to know and they looked away."

"They'll find out" is all he said. And somehow that annoyed me. That he had nothing more to say about that.

~

A few nights later I woke in the middle of the night and was visited by a memory, one I had put out of my head because it was so unpleasant; I had shoved it down to where bad memories become scraps of Kleenex in the bottom of a pocket. But the memory was this:

As part of the book tour I had taken the autumn before all this had occurred—the pandemic, I mean—I had been asked to attend a class at the college I had gone to outside of Chicago. I was to be in Chicago as part of the tour, and so I said yes. But the night before this class I suddenly had a very bad feeling about it. I do not know why. I barely slept that night because my dread continued to grow.

As soon as I walked into the classroom, I felt that my concerns had been true. As the students came in they did not look at me, and I was embarrassed. I was supposed to talk to them about my memoir, which was about growing up poor. But the students would not look at me. And because they would not look at me, I became what I thought they were thinking I was: an old woman who had written about coming from poverty. So I felt cold—emotionally, I mean. Because I thought they saw me that way. I asked each of them where they were from, and each one mumbled the name of a town that I happened to know was a wealthy town. One young woman was from Maine, and she was the only one who even glanced at me. But I thought: This is not the school I went to over forty years ago. And I think it was not. Back then there had not been the sense of wealth I saw sitting in that classroom, in these closed-off young people. They sat around a conference table, there were fifteen of them, and they sat with their shoulders slumped and they would not look at me. As the teacher started to talk—she was a youngish woman with a perky voice—they still did not look at me. She said, "Let's ask Lucy all the questions you have prepared."

But she got nothing out of them. To this day I do not understand what went wrong, but the teacher was unable to get them to talk to me, and for an entire hour we sat in that classroom almost in silence, and I thought: It is like my entire life's work has turned into a small pile of ashes on this table. My humiliation was so deep, it seemed to go straight through all of me into my feet.

One student, a young man from Shaker Heights, said, glancing at me sullenly, "I thought your father was gross." And I thought: Oh God. I said, "Well, he was the product of his time and place in history." And no one said anything.

The teacher said, "Let's tell Lucy the books we have been reading and the ones we have enjoyed so much."

And so she went around the table, and two of the young women named a book that had been on the best-seller list for two years, and others mentioned books I had not heard of. The teacher said, "Lucy, what have you been reading?" And I said that I had been reading biographies of the Russian writers, and I saw then a few of the students smirk.

Finally the teacher said, "Well, okay, then, let's thank Lucy for coming in today." And she started to clap, but no one clapped.

As I left the building with the teacher, she said, "I wish we could have coffee, but I have a meeting to go to."

I could almost not walk to my car, I felt so shaky. They had humiliated me beyond my depths, and I remembered how when one of the young women—she had red hair and small eyes—had mentioned her favorite book being that one on the bestseller list, I had looked at her and I had thought: You will become nothing of worth before climate change kills you.

I had thought that!!!

As I sat in the car in the parking lot, shame poured through me, a shame I had first known in childhood. These students had been exactly like my classmates in grade school who had not looked at me at all. But this time I did not know why. These students—their disdain for me had been so real that remembering it now made my heart start to go much faster. I thought about my niece Lila and the fact that she had made it through only one year of college before she came home, and I felt I understood that now.

. . .

And lying next to William, who was asleep—his slow, steady breathing told me this—and feeling the same degree of humiliation I had felt in that classroom, I thought: I understand those people who went to the Capitol and smashed the windows.

I got up quietly and went downstairs. And I kept thinking about this. I thought: For one hour that day outside of Chicago, I had felt my childhood humiliation so deeply again. And what if I had continued to feel that my entire life, what if all the jobs I had taken in my life were not enough to really make a living, what if I felt looked down upon *all the time* by the wealthier people in this country, who made fun of my religion and my guns. I did not have religion and I did not have guns, but I suddenly felt that I saw what these people were feeling; they were like my sister, Vicky, and I understood them. They had been made to feel poorly about themselves, they were looked at with disdain, and they could no longer stand it.

I sat for a long time on the couch in the dark; there was a half moon that shone over the ocean. And then I thought, No, those were Nazis and racists at the Capitol. And so my understanding—my imagining of the breaking of the windows—stopped there.

~

A few weeks after this I saw Charlene Bibber in the grocery store. "Charlene!" I said, and she said, "Hi, Lucy." I
thought she had gained weight; her eyes looked smaller in
her face.

"How have you been?" I asked her, and she only
shrugged. "Do you want to walk? It's cold, but let's walk,"
I said, and she hesitated and then she said, "Okay."

So we met that Friday by the river and we sat on one of
the granite slabs that we used to sit on, and she asked me,
"Are you still losing your mind?" And I said, Probably. She
said she was definitely losing her mind, and I asked her
how she knew.

Charlene glanced up at a tree branch, and said, "Oh,
look at that." I looked up and there were two black birds
on a bare branch, and one of the birds was sticking its
beak all around the other bird's head, and then down the
other bird's back. Charlene said, "Oh, look, Lucy—he
loves her. He's taking care of her." She dropped her eyes to
look at me then and said, "I know a little bit about birds
because Olive Kitteridge loves birds so much, and one of
the things I learned is that they do take care of each other."
She looked up again and said, "He's probably getting little
bugs off her or something, to keep her wings clean. I read

about that online." She looked at me again, and her eyes shone with an almost-happiness, it seemed to me.

Then another black bird flew over to them from a different tree, and that bird stayed with them for a few minutes before flying back to its own tree. "Uncle Harry just checking on them," Charlene said.

"That's funny," I said.

We watched the birds a while longer, it was an overcast day and their blackness was striking against the gray leafless branch they were on, and behind that the sky was a lighter gray.

Charlene sighed then, and she said, "I'm not going to work at the food pantry anymore."

"Why?" I asked.

"Well." She tugged her coat closer to her and said, "When the vaccines come out—and they're coming—I'm not going to get one, and so I won't be able to work there."

"They told you that?"

"Yup." Charlene picked at one eye with a gloved hand.

I almost said, Why won't you get a vaccine? But I did not say that, and she did not tell me why.

"I'm sorry," I said, and she said, "Thanks."

We sat there in the quiet, and then she said, "Well, let's get walking."

Seven

i

In the middle of January, William received an email saying that he was eligible for the first shot of his vaccine. It named the time and place: 5:30 P.M. at the hospital in town, one week from then. He was eligible because he was over seventy.

I drove so that he could look at his iPad for directions. It was dark, and one of our car's front lights was not working. William told me to put the lights on high because that way they both worked. So I did that, but every so often a car coming toward us would flash its lights at me and I felt terrible, I have always been frightened of doing something wrong, of being inconsiderate; it is a real fear I have.

We got to the hospital, and there was a huge sign that said to drive around to the back, and so we did and then William went in. I waited in the semi-darkness and watched as people went in and out. Some people looked youngish, the way they walked, they were in shape for seventy years or older. Others walked in carefully, many were alone, and I saw a few couples drive up and sit in their cars. In the light of the streetlamps above I could see them fiddling with the papers they had to fill out—as William had had to—and the vulnerability of these people moved me.

William texted that he had had the shot but had to wait ten minutes. And then he came out and we drove home with our bright lights on, and a few people flashed their lights at me, and, again, I felt terrible about that. But William had had his shot. In three weeks he was to go back.

I did not know yet when I would have mine.

And somehow during this time I often felt sad. It was February and it was very cold. I only saw Bob once a week when we bundled up and went for a walk by the river. The days were getting longer, though, and Bob pointed out how at this time of year when the sun was setting it was not "*going away,* the way it felt in December," is what he said, it was "just getting ready for the next day." I saw what he meant, as the sky would break open with a yellow glow as the sun was setting and then shoot pink across the clouds.

. . .

But otherwise I really saw no one else, and William was often on the phone to people he had worked with—or to Lois Bubar's son—and he was very excited about the work he was doing at the university.

Everyone needs to feel important.

I thought again about how my mother—my real one—had said this to me one day. And she was absolutely right. Everyone has to feel like they matter.

I did not feel that I mattered. Because in a way I have never been able to feel that. And so the days were hard.

At night I started once again to wake while it was still dark, and I would lie there and think about my life, and I could make no sense of it. It seemed to come to me in fragments, and the fact that my brother had died, and that my sister had resented me her entire life, sat like a dark wet patch of sand on my soul, and then I would think about when the girls were little, but they were somehow not always happy memories for me, because I seemed only to remember how William had been cheating on me for so many years during that time, and so what I might otherwise have thought of as a good memory was not one.

I thought of how my life had become so different from

what I had ever imagined for myself during these—my last—years. I thought of how I had pictured Christmases with Chrissy and Becka and eventually their children—and David!—in one of their apartments in Brooklyn. But now neither child lived there, and neither would probably ever return.

I thought of how I would live out my days in this house on a small cliff on the coast of Maine with William, how Bridget would come to us in the summers; perhaps she would even come for a Christmas, how did I know?

I wondered if I had become too frightened to return to New York again. It was funny, but I felt that in my enclosed world I had somehow become worse about that—about my fears, I mean.

I could not stop feeling that life as I had known it was gone.

Because it was.

I knew this was true.

I told Bob about that as we walked one day in late February by the river. The day was not terribly cold, and the river was not frozen as it had been. Bob walked with his hands in his pockets and looked at me sideways, his mask covering most of his face. "What do you mean?" he asked, and I tried to explain how I had always been a frightened person, and how I was afraid now that when and if I ever got back to New York, how would I do it? I said I was no longer young, and Bob said, "I know." But then he said, "It's funny that you call yourself a frightened person. I think of you as brave."

"Are you *kidding*?" I said. I stopped walking to look at him.

"Not a bit," he said. "Think about your life. You came from really hard circumstances, you left a marriage that was not working, you wrote books that have really reached people. You married another guy who was wonderful to you. Sorry, Lucy, but that's not what frightened people do." He started to walk again. "But I know what you mean about New York. Margaret hates the place, so she no longer makes the trip with me, but I've been thinking how when I finally get my shot, what will it be like?"

It was quite a walk that day.

Bob spoke of his brother, Jim, who lived in Brooklyn with his wife, Helen. Bob had not seen them in over a year, though Jim had just gotten his first shot. Bob said to me, "Honestly, Lucy?" He sat down on a granite seat so he could have his cigarette. He pulled a cigarette from the pack and lit it, then put the pack back into his pocket. He exhaled and said, "Jim has kind of been the love of my life. How strange is that?" He looked at me. "I mean, I have just loved that guy so much, and he did break my heart, but I have just always—I don't know—he's like the furnace that has kept me going."

"Oh Bob," I said. "Oh God, I get it."

"I mean, when Pam left I was a mess." He told me how he had moved to a fourth-floor walkup in Brooklyn to be near his brother, and how Jim had made fun of the place, calling it a "graduate dorm." Bob said he drank too much during those days, he didn't like to think about them now, and then he had finally moved to a doorman building on the Upper West Side of Manhattan. "And to *really* tell you the truth?" He shook his head as he took another drag on his cigarette. "To tell you the absolute truth, I wish Pam had never left. Oh Lucy, I wish she could have had her kids with me. I miss her, and I think she still misses me."

"She does," I said. "I saw her at William's seventieth birthday party and she told me that she still thinks of you."

Bob kept shaking his head. "Boy. It makes me sad. I think she's okay, she's got her kids and everything, and we talk once in a while. But it's a sad story, Lucy. Both Pam and Jim are in New York and they always will be, and I will always be here in Maine."

We sat in silence while I absorbed this. Oh, he broke my heart!

．　．　．

After a while we began to talk again. I told him that I sus-
pected that William and I were together now until the very
end, and that I was glad—but that somehow there was an
uncertainty for me.

Bob squinted at me. "What's the uncertainty, Lucy?"

"I don't really know." I shifted my legs and said, "But
he loves it up here now. He's got his 'sister' "—I put my
fingers up in quotes as I said that—"and he loves her,
which is good. But he's *really* excited about what he's
doing at the University of Maine now, and they seem excited about him there, so I don't know—I mean I don't
know what will happen when this is all over.

"He mentioned his apartment in New York to me the
other day, as though I would go there with him whenever
we went to New York. But I told him no, that had been his
apartment with Estelle, I was not going to stay there—
which makes sense to me—but he seemed slightly surprised by that."

Bob said, "Well, Lucy." And he looked me straight in
the eye. "Speaking for myself, I would love it more than
anything if you stayed here in this town."

He said that to me.

He made me feel that I mattered. Bob Burgess was the
only person who seemed able to do that for me right now.

ii

By early March a number of things had happened:

I had finished my Arms Emory story. The story has Arms finding out that Jimmie Wagg is selling Legs his drugs, and all Arms wants to do is go find Jimmie Wagg.

Arms finds the three young men down by one of the abandoned cottages I had seen in Dixon along the river through the trees, and as Arms is kneeing Jimmie to get him into the cruiser, Sperm runs up and with his small spiky teeth bites Arms on the calf, and this inflames Arms so much that he picks Sperm up and, with his strong arms, and without even meaning to, breaks the kid's skinny neck.

The story ends with a flash into the future: that Arms would retire from the police force, and that he would visit Sperm every single day—Sperm sitting in his wheelchair with a ventilator—in the squalid home Sperm lived in alone with his mother, and that Arms would end up loving Sperm as he had loved his own brother, shaving him gently as his whiskers started to grow on his cheeks, clipping his fingernails for him too.

· · ·

That night I said to William, who was reading a book, "My Arms Emory story is sympathetic toward a white cop who liked the old president and who does an act of violence and gets away with it. Maybe I shouldn't publish it right now."

William looked up and said, "Well, it might help people understand each other. Just publish it, Lucy."

I was quiet for a long time. Then I said, "I used to tell my students to write against the grain. Meaning: Try to go outside your comfort level, because that's where interesting things will happen on the page."

William kept reading his book. He said, "Just put the story out there."

But I knew I could not trust myself—or other people. But mostly I could not trust myself: to know what to *do* these days. I knew that many people understood what was right and what was wrong, but these days I could not fully understand that myself. *Mom!* I called to my nice made-up mother, and she said, You'll figure it out, Lucy, you always do.

I did not know if that was true.

But I felt very sad about Arms Emory; I loved him.

iii

And then I had both my vaccines, three weeks apart. When the woman put the needle into my arm for the second shot, I almost wept. I thought: I am free. I thought: I will see New York again.

William and I made a plan. I would take a train by myself to New Haven and spend a night with Chrissy and also a night with Becka in her new apartment there, and then I would go into the city for a week. William would fly down and visit with Estelle and Bridget during this time, before coming to meet me. The girls would come into the city and visit me separately, they had said this, and I had found that slightly strange, I mean that they would come separately.

And then William would meet me there, and the girls would come back to see him. I made a reservation—or William made it for me—for an Airbnb in New York.

～

While we waited for the three weeks to go by until my vaccine was all set inside me, Becka called and said that she had been accepted at Yale Law School. In truth, I was shocked by this. William did not seem shocked. "We always knew she was smart," he said. And that was true. But Becka at Yale? In law school?

Becka added, "Don't make a big deal out of it when you speak to Chrissy."

And this surprised me again. Chrissy had gone to Brooklyn Law School, and I had never picked up on any competition between them. Chrissy was the older, in some ways she was bossy, and she had—in her youth—sort of bossed Becka around, which Becka—for the most part— had seemed to take easily.

So when I spoke to Chrissy on the phone, I did not mention it, and I noticed that she did not mention it as well. Chrissy sounded distracted enough that I asked if she was all right, and she said, "God, Mom. Please. Of *course* I am."

"Well, I will see you soon," I said, and she only said "See you soon," and hung up.

I sat for quite a while after that phone call.

Eight

i

And so it was the first week in April that William drove me to South Station in Boston to put me on a train to New Haven. What I noticed as we drove into Boston was that there were places to park on the street. And that the sky was so blue. *So* blue! "From not having any traffic for a year," William said. He found a parking place not far from the station and we got out and he wheeled my little suitcase behind him; the city seemed to sparkle in the sunshine and the blue of that sky.

But when we stepped into the train station, I was astonished. There was the sense of a war having occurred. One that was not yet over. The lights were very low. And every single shop in the station was closed except for a doughnut place that was only selling coffee, and the woman who was selling it had her little girl next to her sitting on a wooden crate; the schools were still closed. "William," I whispered. "I know," he said.

A policeman stood watch.

To one side were benches, and on these benches were homeless people, many were sleeping, others were just staring, their bags of newspapers and clothes near them. One older woman who—to my eyes—did not look homeless rose from her bench and began walking through the station. She was wearing a kind of pretty dress, and she talked as she walked; I thought she might be on the phone, but as she passed by me I saw that she was not on any phone. "I went inside the place to see if I could get a roll." This is what I heard her saying.

William walked me onto the train because the conductor let him, and the conductor said to us, "Ninety percent of the people working for this railroad got the virus." She added, "But I didn't. I was super, super careful, I have a compromised child at home." Then she continued down the aisle, and William had to leave. He stood outside my window and waved. I began to feel a sense of nothingness, which is the only way I can explain it.

There were others on the train. Across the aisle from me sat a young woman who was reading a book, and every so often she would glance over and smile at me. And there was a man a few rows ahead of me; every time the conductor went by she said to this man, "Put the mask over your nose," and he always apologized.

I sat and looked out the window, but I could not feel much.

And then finally the train pulled into New Haven.

~

The first thing was this: I got off the train and looked around, and it was not until she walked toward me that I recognized my daughter Chrissy.

She had become skinny again. Not as skinny as when she had been sick, years ago after William and I split up, but she was thin.

"Hi, Mom," she said, and we hugged, and I said, "Chrissy—"

And she said, "What?" She was wearing jeans that were tight, and her long legs seemed to go on and on.

"You're skinny again, honey," I said.

"I've been working out a lot." She held up her arm and showed me her small muscle through her tight shirt.

"But, Chrissy—"

"Mom, *don't*," she said. "Do not talk to me about my weight."

. . .

"Where's Becka?" I asked, and Chrissy said, "Waiting for you in her apartment." And so we drove there. Chrissy seemed very much in charge, as though she were a president or a CEO—this went through my head—and when we got to Becka's little place, not far from Yale, Chrissy pulled over and said, "She's on the second floor. See you tomorrow."

"Tomorrow?" I asked. "I thought we'd all be together for dinner tonight."

"No, you need to see her alone. Bye, Mom." And she drove away.

Becka came running down the stairs and threw open the door and said, *"Mom!"* She put her arms around me and said, "We can hug, Mom!" And we hugged. Oh my dear sweet Becka. She went ahead of me up the stairs, dragging my violet-colored little suitcase, and her apartment was small but adorable. She had her bed in an alcove, and she had a piece of cloth on that wall, with all her jewelry hanging on it. Earrings, necklaces. It was very her.

"Mommy, how are you?" She asked this, throwing herself onto the couch and patting the place next to her. "Tell me everything."

And so we talked, and she was very excited about starting law school in the fall. She was still doing her social
work for the city, still doing it from home, and she told me
what she hoped to do with her law degree, which was to
go into "policy," as she put it, and I listened, and she
looked beautiful to me.

Then I asked her about her sister. "She's gotten skinny
again," I said. And Becka's face changed, she looked away
from me, and then she said with a big sigh, "Mom, Chrissy's going through a rough patch, that's all I'm allowed to
say."

"A rough patch? What kind of rough patch?"

"Mom." Becka looked at me with her large brown eyes.
"I'm not supposed to tell you, so I'm not going to."

It was hard, after that, to enjoy myself. But Becka
cooked us dinner and she talked and talked, and she was
so Becka; she did make me happy.

"You sleep on my bed, I'll sleep on the couch," she said,
and she dragged a quilt from a closet and got the couch all
made up, and I said, "That looks really cozy, actually,"
and she said, "You want to sleep there? Sleep wherever you
want, Mom. Seriously."

So I slept on the couch, and I was surprised that I
slept—but it is because of Becka that I did. She really did
make the world seem like a cozy place. In the morning she

said, "Okay, so in four days I will come into the city and we will see each other again, and then when Dad gets there, I'll come back and see him too."

We hugged and hugged as Chrissy sat behind the wheel of her car waiting for me to get in.

ii

When I stepped into Chrissy and Michael's house, I was surprised to find that I had the reaction I always have to the houses of other people. I mean, I did not like it. I had been inside this house a couple of times before when Michael's parents had lived in it; David had been there with me as well, once, when Chrissy became engaged to Michael. But stepping through the side door now, watching the thin legs of my daughter as she went before me, I felt a sense of dismalness.

The house seemed terribly grown up. The curtains that hung at the windows were beige with golden-colored strips weaving through them. The sun came through the window of the kitchen, which made the refrigerator and the stove—both aluminum-seeming—gleam. The table was dark wood, and I thought: This is not unlike Catherine's house, Chrissy's grandmother. When I first saw Catherine's house, I was still practically a child, and I was astonished by the beauty of it. But this did not astonish me, it depressed me.

Michael walked into the kitchen and said, "Hi, Lucy, so nice to see you," and we hugged. I felt his arms on my back; he was really hugging me.

Michael made dinner while Chrissy and I sat at the table and talked. She spoke mostly of her work with the ACLU, and I thought: She is not talking about anything real. And I think by that I mean that she was not talking about how she felt, but she was pleasant and we all ate dinner at their dark table, and I did notice that Chrissy had just a salad and three glasses of red wine. Afterward they took me upstairs to their spare bedroom and we all said goodnight.

A few hours later I heard Chrissy speak to Michael in a voice I would never have thought could be hers. She said, "I don't *believe* you couldn't even take the garbage out!" She did not know I heard, I had stepped out of my room to get a glass of water in the bathroom to take a sleeping tablet, and standing at the top of the stairs I heard her in the kitchen saying this to Michael, and her voice was so terribly—unbelievably—harsh. Michael only murmured something, and then I heard a cupboard door slam and I went into the bathroom quietly.

I thought to myself: She has lost all respect for him.

But in the morning, she drove me to the train station, and she said, all smiles, "Okay, enjoy New York, I will see you there in two days!"

Michael had just said goodbye at the door, quiet, as he often was. I had hugged him goodbye, and he did not hug me as hard as he had when I'd arrived.

The train ride into the city seemed interminable. I could not stop thinking about Chrissy. I thought: The girl is forty years old, if she gets really skinny-sick she could die. I thought: Something is wrong in her marriage.

~

It was a sunny day, and as the train got closer to the city, I felt a very small—but real—sense of excitement, just looking out the windows of the train and seeing more and more buildings—and people, too, who were sometimes sitting on their tiny terraces that looked out over the train tracks. All this made me feel almost happy.

But when we pulled into the city itself I could see in the distance the building I had once lived in. And I did not feel anything. And I continued to feel that way as I got out at Grand Central, which felt eerily empty to me; only a few of us walked through it, and all the stores in it were closed. And then there were no taxis, as I had thought there might not be. So I walked around the station, and on the other side was one taxi and he took me to where I was staying.

An emptiness had come into me.

iii

The Airbnb was in midtown, and there were lace curtains on the windows, and it was on the first floor of a brownstone. I had lived in a brownstone in Brooklyn years earlier and I had forgotten that one could not see much from inside, but these curtains made me feel like I was inside a coffin. When I had moved to Manhattan I had always lived high up in a building, and I had always had a view of parts of the city. So I felt even stranger as I walked through the two rooms, and when William called me I could not explain to him what I was feeling. But I told him about Chrissy, and his voice dropped and he said, "Oh God, Lucy."

There was a small circular shower with a curtain around it, and as I took a shower I thought I might fall; that is how disoriented I felt.

For two days I walked through the city; I had not told any of my friends that I would be there, I had thought I would

surprise them and then go see them, but I was glad now
that no one knew I was here. I did not feel that I could give
them the attention they deserved. I noticed that there were
very few taxicabs around. Clothing stores that had lined a
whole section of Lexington Avenue were shut, some with
a kind of peeling white paper on the insides of their windows.

I walked across Park Avenue against the light; that is how
few cars were on the street.

I sat in Central Park and saw the flowering bushes and the
leaves that were already out and I watched people go by,
there were many people. But I felt nothing.

I went back to Grand Central on Monday morning at nine
o'clock, and as I stood on the balcony looking down, there
was only one man walking through the wide stretch of the
station as above him was the large ceiling with its constel-
lations.

In the afternoon I went to Bloomingdale's to get some
perfume—I have a particular scent I always use—and so I
went to the area on the first floor with all the different
makeup places, and I bought a small bottle that I would

be able to take home on the airplane—we were going to fly back—and I noticed that the salesclerk did not try and sell me anything else, which was different, usually they would say, "Are you *sure* you don't want to try some of this new night cream?" Or something like that. But this salesclerk just hurriedly sold me the perfume and then she said, Oh, here, and she handed me a bag of little samples of makeup that one usually gets after one spends enough money, and my small perfume had not been enough to do that, but she shoved the bag at me and I thanked her and she said, "Sure."

And then I could not find my way out of the store. I kept wandering through the huge makeup section, starting one way, thinking, This is not right, and turning around and going in the other direction and thinking, No, this is not right, and finally a salesman approached me with his black mask on and he said, Can I help you? And I said, I want to get out of the store. And he so courteously ushered me out.

~

That night as I lay awake in the Airbnb, I thought of all the people—old people and young people—who had lived out the pandemic in rooms like I was in right now. Alone.

iv

I went to meet Chrissy in Central Park, we had arranged to meet at the duck pond, and she was already there when I arrived. She waved; she had sunglasses on. "Hi, honey," I said, sitting down next to her on a bench, and she said, "Hi, Mom. One second. Hold on." And she texted someone and then looked at me and said, "So how does New York seem to you?"

"Oh, it's strange," I told her.

"Yeah? How so?"

Something was really wrong with my child.

A woman who was perhaps fifty years old kept walking quickly around the duck pond. She was on a cellphone and I heard her speaking Italian. Around and around she went in an outfit of dark green workout pants and a workout jacket the same color. She wore a bright orange mask, pulled down below her chin.

As we sat on the bench, Chrissy kept looking at her phone. At one point she said, "Sorry, Mom, I just have to answer this," and she typed away furiously and then finally put her phone away. She seemed to relax just a little bit.

And then I had a vision: Chrissy was having an affair. Or she was about to have an affair.

I looked straight ahead while she talked, she was talking about her work, some sort of internal trouble the organization was having but her own job was perfectly safe, it was just interesting to watch these other people go after each other. Something like that she was saying.

And I said, "Chrissy, don't do it."

I turned to look at her, and she took her sunglasses off and looked me straight in the eye, her eyes are hazel, and I felt I had never looked at her so hard, or she at me. "Do what?" she finally said.

And I said, "Do not have that affair."

And she kept looking at me; her eyes above her mask became tighter, it seemed to me. She would not look away. Then she began to complain about Michael. She said, "You have no idea what he's really like, Mom. You never did. You know what he does for a living, Mom? He manages people's money—how meaningful is that?"

"Pretty meaningful," I said, "to those who have money."

She got angrier. "Right. Well, there are millions and millions of people in this world without money, so ask them how meaningful it is."

"But you knew that when you married him."

She opened her mouth and closed it, and I realized then

that when a person is having an affair, their spouse becomes demonized. This is the way it is.

But when she said *this* to me, I almost died.

Chrissy said, and her voice started to tremble, "Mom, you have no idea how fucked up it got me when you said that you and Dad were back together. You just said it, like it was nothing! You just blithely said it— *Mom,* you don't get it, do you? You just tell us that after all this time oh by the way you and Dad got back together, as if all that *shit* that you guys went through together—that *affected* us, I might add!—that all that *crap* was all of a sudden no big deal, and—" She gave an exaggerated shrug, throwing her arms up slightly, she was really angry. "Just like that, oh we're back together."

We sat in silence for many moments.

"Did you have another miscarriage?" I finally asked her.

Chrissy said, "Who told you? Did Becka tell you that?"

"Nobody told me anything. I'm just asking."

Chrissy put her sunglasses on again and stretched her thin legs out in front of her; her arms were crossed. "Yeah, I did," she said. "In the middle of January."

"Oh Chrissy." I put my hand on her leg but she did not respond. We sat like that in the sun for some time. Then I said quietly, "Chrissy, this is about loss. You've lost three pregnancies and you're angry. That's really understand-able. But don't blow your marriage up over it. Please, Chrissy. Please don't do that."

She said, quietly, "Well, you did that. You said you had an affair and it got you out of your marriage to Dad."

"That's right," I said. "And I wish now neither of us had had any affairs."

She looked at me through her sunglasses. She was very angry. She said, "You were adored by a husband, Mom. David *adored* you. He *adored* you! And now you're telling me you wish you hadn't met him? How crazy is that?"

I shook my head slowly. I had nothing to say to her accusation.

Eventually I said, "Is this man married?"

And Chrissy said, "Mom, where have you been? How do you even know it's a man? It could be a woman, or a gender-nonconforming individual."

I said, "It's a *woman*?"

She looked at me angrily and said, "No, it's a man. I'm just asking where you've been the last couple of years. We don't make *assumptions* like that anymore."

Then I said, "Are there little kids?" And she said nothing. "Oh Chrissy," I said. "I'm so sorry, honey. God, am I sorry."

After a moment she turned to me and said, "Okay, the

truth is we haven't done it yet, but so what. We just haven't been able to get away, but we're working on it. I'm seeing him tomorrow, as a matter of fact."

I looked at her and I said, "Honestly, Chrissy? I could be sick right now. This has made me sick."

She said, "It's not always about you, Mom."

After a long silence I said, "Chrissy, you need to be seeing a therapist about this. Are you?"

In a moment, she shook her head to indicate no.

Rapidly—and unexpectedly—I remembered that last dream I had had of my father after he died, when I had said to him, "It's okay, Daddy, I can drive the truck now."

Because, bizarrely, I felt that my head was becoming extremely clear after so long of its feeling not quite right.

I turned so that I was facing Chrissy. "You listen to me," I said. "You listen to every single word I have to tell you. And take your sunglasses off. I need to see your face."

She took her sunglasses off. But she did not look at me.

"I would never have left your father if he had not had those affairs. I know that about myself. I would never have had an affair myself if he had not had all those that he did. So that's the first thing. The second thing is, I know this is about loss. Because when I had my disgusting little affair—and it *was* disgusting—I had lost my mother, and then my father. And then the next year you went off to college, and Becka was getting ready to go. And my psychiatrist said to me, she said to me, Lucy, this is about *loss*. And you, Chrissy, you have had loss. You have lost three babies, and now you think that you have lost your mother because I am back with your father."

Chrissy turned to look at me then. She looked at me with interest.

"And I'm going to tell you one more thing. When I met that man—the man I had that affair with that made me realize I could no longer live with your father—we were at a writers' conference, and he came on to me, and he made me feel special. That's what he did. It was pretty simple when I look back: He just showered me with attention and made me feel very special at a time when I felt not so special."

"You never feel special," Chrissy said, but she said it quietly and not meanly, I thought.

"You're right, I don't. But I was feeling especially not special with all my own losses, and he paid great attention to me. And email had just started up back then, and every day he emailed me, imploring me, and every day I wrote back: No. And then this happened:

"I went out for dinner with a woman I had met years earlier. She was one of the saddest women I have ever known. She had never had a boyfriend or a girlfriend, and God knows she would have told me if she had. She was *sad*, Chrissy, she was damaged in some fundamental way; she had never had a day of therapy, she just lived her life as a tax attorney, and we went out for dinner that night, and then I realized that she probably was an alcoholic. She had at least a bottle of wine that night, and a martini to start off with, and then— Are you listening?"

But I could tell she was. She was watching me with real interest on her face. She nodded.

"And then, for dessert, she ordered these special-made doughnuts that came with chocolate sauce you could dip them in, and as I watched her dipping these little dough-nuts in this chocolate sauce I felt such a sense—I guess a sense of fear—because I was in the presence of such deep loneliness. And I thought, Yes, I am going to have that af-fair.

"And so I went home and wrote him just the word Yes. And he was ecstatic. And that was that."

Chrissy turned her face to look out over the pond, and she let out a deep breath.

"But I have always thought that if I had not had dinner with that sad, sad woman that night I would not have given in to him. And so now you ask about David. And yes, David adored me, and I adored him. But was it worth it? There's no way of judging that, Chrissy. But you see the pain that Trey caused Becka—"

"I see that she got out of a marriage she didn't want," Chrissy said, turning back to look at me.

I thought about that. "Okay," I said. "But she married Trey on the rebound. And you did not." I added, "Her marriage was different from the one you have with Michael. When you met Michael through those mutual friends, you just clicked, Chrissy, everyone could see it. And you would laugh together, remember at your wedding how that guy who gave a toast said he would hear you both laughing and laughing in the hallway of some place?"

I waited a moment, squinting at the duck pond, and then I turned back to her. "Have you told Michael any of this?"

She shook her head quickly.

"But you're obviously not getting along. Because you want to be with someone else. Or you think you do. So listen to me more, Chrissy. This is important. Do not put this on Michael. You make the decision of what you're going to do, but you do not need to tell him that you're attracted to someone else. I suspect he knows this and he feels humiliated and has no idea what to do because everything he does right now you find abhorrent. If you want to leave the marriage, then leave the marriage. But if you don't, then try to be more openhearted to your husband."

As soon as I said this I realized she could not do that. So I said, "But I suspect you can't do that, be openhearted to him now, because you don't want him."

Chrissy, who had been looking at me intently, looked away. I watched the side of her face, and she seemed no longer angry; there was a vulnerability to her face, is what I am saying.

I put my hand on her arm. After a few moments, she put her hand on mine briefly, and when she looked at me there were tears in her eyes and they began to slip down her face. She rubbed them away with the back of her hand. "Oh honey," I said. "Honey, honey, honey."

I waited to see if she would cry harder, and she did—briefly—and then she stopped.

"Okay, I hear you," she said, and she stood up.

And then she began to sob—oh, that child sobbed!—and she sat back down and I put my arms around her, and she let me, and we sat there for a very long time while she cried and cried and cried and I kept my arms around her, sometimes kissing her head, which she had tucked down under my chin.

The Italian-speaking woman walked past us again.

V

I did not speak of this exchange to William that night, although I was desperate to tell him; he was staying with Estelle and Bridget out in Larchmont for two nights, he had just arrived, and then he was going back to his apartment for the first time, and I could hear in his voice how preoccupied he was with these things and so I thought: I will tell him when he gets here.

~

I lay on the bed with the lace curtains near me. But all I could think of was Chrissy.

Oh child!

Who was no longer a child—

~

I thought about William's affairs, and I will tell you this about finding out about them:

It humbled me. It humbled me unbelievably. It brought me to my knees. And I was humbled because I had not known such a thing could happen in my own life. I had thought that this sort of thing happened to other women.

I remember going to a party during this period, and I overheard two women talking about a woman whose husband had had an affair. And what I remember—*it scorched me*—was how both women said, Oh, come on, how could she not have known?

And then it happened to me.

And when I found out I had been living a parallel life, a dishonest life, it crushed me. But I have often thought that it made me a nicer person, I really do. When you are truly humbled, that can happen. I have come to notice this in life. You can become bigger or bitter, this is what I think. And as a result of that pain, I became bigger. Because I understood then how a woman could not know. It had happened, and it had happened to me.

Because I would never have had an affair, I thought William would not either.

I had been thinking like myself.

Lying there on the bed with the lace curtains at the window, I thought how it had become a sort of private joke between David and me, the thinking-like-yourself line. If David wondered, let's say, why the conductor of the Philharmonic eviscerated the new violinist one night, I would say, "You're thinking like yourself, David." And he would laugh and agree. "Get inside his head, and you might understand," I'd say, and David would say that he didn't want to be inside that man's head.

Everyone thinks like themselves, this is my point.

And then as I turned over in the bed, I thought about what Chrissy had said about David adoring me. She was right, he did adore me.

Would I really have given that up?

It did not matter at this point; my life had unfolded as it had.

And hers would unfold too, in whatever way it did.

~

The next day my head stayed clear. I told myself: There is nothing you can do about it. (But in truth, I felt afraid for my child.)

I walked the streets of the city, and I noticed that if someone stepped in front of me on the sidewalk, they said "Oh, sorry," or "Excuse me." This happened a number of times. The man in the deli who made my sandwich for lunch told me to have a really good day. "A *really* good one, okay?" And he smiled as he gave me my sandwich.

On many doors of places that were open were signs that said, We Are All In This Together.

~

William called and said that Estelle and Bridget were moving back to the city soon, Estelle had had her vaccination and they seemed to be doing okay. But he sounded solemn and I waited and he said, "I'm calling from outside their place, and I'll go to my apartment tomorrow. I dread it, Lucy."

I still wanted to speak to him about Chrissy, but I did not want him thinking about that while he was with Bridget, and so I did not tell him.

"How's Bridget?" I asked, and his voice became lighter and he said, "She's good. It's been great to be able to see her."

He said that when he came into the city in two days he'd have to go to his office and hopefully see some people and get his retirement stuff in order and visit his lab for the last time, and I understood that this made him sad. So for these reasons I did not tell him that Chrissy—probably as we spoke—was meeting with a man she planned to have an affair with. I just reminded him that I was seeing Becka tomorrow and that both girls would come back in a few days and see him with me as well.

"Okay, Lucy." He did not say he loved me as we hung up, as David would always do. But William wasn't David. That much I knew. And he didn't have to be. I knew that too.

～

That night as I got ready for bed I got a text from Chrissy. It said: I'm coming into the city tomorrow with Becka to see you again.

I wrote back: I'm glad.

～

And there they were, my beautiful daughters. By the duck pond were my two girls. But they were never really mine, I thought as I walked toward them, any more than New York City was ever really mine. These two thoughts went through my head. Chrissy and Becka put their hands up and waved as I walked down the little hill. The sun was shining again, although clouds were moving in. Neither of the girls was wearing sunglasses, and so I slipped mine into my coat pocket as I approached. After I had hugged them both they moved apart so that I could sit between them. Chrissy was holding a large paper cup with a top on it—coffee, I supposed. She took a sip from it. She looked tired to me.

I waited.

Chrissy said, "Okay, just so you know. And, by the way, Becka knows all about this." Chrissy sat up straighter and looked at me. "I went to see that guy yesterday."

"And?" I asked this after a moment.

"And, Mom, he made a huge, huge mistake with me." Chrissy drew her fingers through her hair. "When I told him I wasn't sure if I wanted to go through with this he got furious with me. Mom! He got *really* angry, Mom. *Really, really* angry. It was—honestly?—it was scary, and I thought, God!"

She looked at me, her mouth partly open, her eyes wide.

I said, "So that's it?"

"Oh *God*, yes, that's it." She sat back.

I turned to look at Becka, who only raised her eyebrows at me.

Chrissy said, "And then I went home, and Michael and I had a long talk, and I said I'd been an asshole because of the pregnancies and that I was really sorry, and he was pretty nice. Hesitant, but nice." Here Chrissy's eyes welled up, and I felt Becka's hand squeeze my knee slightly as I watched Chrissy.

I understood that I had no idea what would happen to Chrissy's marriage.

Chrissy said, "It's because I'm old, Mom, and the doctor just doesn't care. He doesn't *care*. And he's supposed to be a specialist."

"Then we'll find you a new doctor. New York is filled with doctors."

She said, "I'm afraid they'll shoot me up with progesterone or something, and that increases my chances of cancer later. I've researched this online."

"Online," I said. "You're getting your medical information online. Well, that may be true. Or not. But we're going to get you to a new doctor. Your father should know one, he knows people in the sciences. Come on, Chrissy. For heaven's sake, this is not over."

"I don't know . . ." she said.

"Well, we'll find out."

Briefly she touched my hand, and as she pulled it away I took her hand in mine, and she let me. We sat in the sun holding hands.

After a few moments Becka asked me, "Mom, so you're going to live the rest of your life up there on a cliff in Maine?"

"I know," I said, turning my face to her. "I know exactly what you're asking. I've been wondering that myself."

Becka said, "Well, it's a cute house. I mean, it could be worse."

"Oh God, it could be a lot worse," I said. Then I said, "Your father loves it there because of his new family and all the parasites and potatoes—"

"I know," Chrissy interrupted. "That's all he talks about when he calls these days."

I thought, Oh God, William. But I continued, "So your father is happy there, and I've made some friends. Bob Burgess for one, I think he's one of the best friends I've ever had." I described him briefly, his sweet bigness, his baggy jeans.

Chrissy looked at me then, and she smiled almost playfully. "Are you going to have an affair, Mom?"

"No," I said seriously. "He's married to a minister, she's a good woman, I think he's a little afraid of her—"

"Why?" Becka interrupted this time.

"Well, he sneaks cigarettes when she's not around."

Chrissy actually laughed at this. And Becka said, "Wait—how old is this guy?"

"Oh, my age I'd say."

"And he has to sneak cigarettes behind his wife's back?"

"Yup," I said.

"Mom, that's crazy."

"Well," I said, "you know, we all make our choices." But as I said that I wondered if it was true—if we really did make our choices—and I thought of that thing I had seen on my computer one night about there being no free will and that everything was predetermined. So I said, "I guess we make our own choices, I don't really know."

Chrissy turned to look at me. "What do you mean? Mom, you just sat here the other day talking me out of a choice I probably would have made, so how can you say you don't really know if we make our own choices?"

"I don't know," I said. "I don't know if I believe it or not." I paused. "I don't really know anything." I added, "Except how much I love you and Becka. I know that."

Chrissy looked straight ahead. "Mom," she said softly, "you know a lot."

Becka spoke again. "Well, we were just thinking— Okay, I'll just say it. We wondered if Dad manipulated you into going up there for the pandemic to get you back with him so he doesn't ever have to be alone again."

"Seriously?" I was really surprised, and then I remembered how Lauren, Becka's therapist, had told Becka years ago that William manipulated me, and how I had never understood it.

I said to them, "He took me up there to save my life. He got you guys out of the city hoping to save your lives as well."

"Oh, we know he loves us," Becka said. She added, "And we love him. But why did he take you to Maine and not somewhere else? Probably because of Lois Bubar, and *that* worked out for him."

I felt a tiny sense of alarm go through me, because I had had that thought myself, after William had met with Lois the first time.

Becka continued, "And you know that saying: Women grieve, and men replace." After a moment she said thoughtfully, "I'm just not sure Dad's always trustworthy."

"In what way, exactly . . . ?" I started to ask.

But then Chrissy suddenly said this: "I'm *hungry*."

She said that!

I stood up and said, "Let's find a place to eat." So we left the park, the sun had come out brightly again, and on Madison Avenue was a place with tables outside, and we sat down in the sunshine and Chrissy looked at the menu and then she said to the waiter, "I'll have a chicken salad sandwich."

"Me too," I said. And Becka shrugged and said, "Okay, then. I will too."

We sat there talking, and after a few moments Chrissy said, "That coffee made me have to pee," so she went in-

side with her mask on, and while she was in there Becka
said to me, "Mom, the guy had blackheads on his nose."

"What guy?" I asked, looking around.

"Chrissy's guy—the guy she was thinking of having sex
with. When she saw him yesterday he had blackheads on
his nose. And then he got really, really pissed at her."

I looked at Becka, who looked back with a shake of her
head. "She said she hadn't seen the blackheads on Zoom."
Becka added, "But it wasn't because of them she didn't do
it. I mean they didn't *help*. It's because he got so scarily
mad at her."

I said, "Thank God," and Becka said, "Right?"

And then Chrissy came back and the sandwiches arrived and I watched Chrissy eat hers—slowly, but she kept
eating it. When she was done with the first half, she looked
at her plate and said, "Well, I might as well," and she
picked up the second half.

God, this relieved me.

I opened my mouth then, because I was just about to say,
Kids, listen. Your father had cancer. But I stopped myself;
I thought how he had not told them, and so I should not
either. And just as I was thinking this, Becka said, mus-
ingly, "It seems like Dad always needs to have secrets."

I was taken aback, and after a moment I said, "What
kind of secrets?"

Becka shrugged and said, "Well, I don't really know specifically anymore. It's just that's why we're a little bit worried about you being back with him."

I paused, considering this. "I don't know if he has any secrets left. And honestly, girls? It doesn't matter anymore. He and I are not young, we're not going to be young again. And we get along fine."

"Just fine?" Chrissy asked.

"Well, more than fine. I know who he is now—I mean, to the extent that anyone in the world can know him."

The girls nodded. "All right," Becka said, just as Chrissy said, "Okay, Mom. As long as you're happy."

So we sat there at our table on the sidewalk—the sun shining down on us as though it would shine on forever—and we talked more, and then finally we left, and the girls went to get their train back to New Haven; they would come back in a few days to see their father. We hugged on the sidewalk. "Bye, Mom," they both said this as their Uber pulled up to the curb, and they stepped into the car.

I stood for a moment, watching them drive away. I thought how different they—and their lives—had become from what I had expected. And I thought: It is their life, they can do what they want, or need to do.

. . .

And then I remembered that one time, when I was pregnant with Chrissy, I had looked down at my big stomach
and put my hand over it and thought: Whoever you are,
you do not belong to me. My job is to help you get into the
world, but you do not belong to me.

And remembering this now, I thought: Lucy, you were absolutely right.

VI

When I got back to the place I was staying in, William
called, filled with sadness about his lab and his apartment,
and then he said, "Lucy, can I come over and spend the
night with you? I don't want to stay in this apartment tonight."

"Of course you can!" I said. "I have *tons* of things to
tell you!"

~

I thought then about how when I first met William he had
taken me on dates. He would take me to a real restaurant!

I had never ever been to a real restaurant. And he would pay for me—so easily, he pulled out his cash and paid for me. And then we would see a movie. Once a week we did this. A movie! I had never seen movies in movie theaters until I went to college, but we would go each Friday night, to dinner and a movie, and he would toss a piece of popcorn into my face as the movie began.

This man had brought me into the world, is what I am saying. As much as I could be brought into the world, William had done this for me.

And yet I could not get Becka's words out of my head: that her father was not trustworthy. I wondered what I had done, agreeing to live in Maine, with his new family now preoccupying him so much, and how I had given up my home in New York.

And then I remembered this: When I lived with William and the girls in Brooklyn, we had a little porch off our bedroom on the second floor, and one morning William found that a squirrel had made a big nest right there on the side of the porch, and he spoke to me about it, and he had decided, I think I decided with him, that the nest would have to go. It was too close to the house. And so William had taken a broom and swept the whole thing away.

And what I remembered is this: that for an entire day and night, and straight through the next day, that squirrel made the sound of crying. The squirrel had cried and cried and cried. Because its home had been taken away.

~

I looked around at the lace curtains on the windows and I thought: *Mom, I don't know who to trust!* And my mother—the nice one I have made up over the years—said to me immediately: Lucy, you trust yourself.

~

I went outside and sat on the stoop of the place I was staying in. I sat there thinking about the girls and William, and David—how gone he was—and how we would all be gone someday. It was not that I was sad as I thought this, I just understood it to be true.

And then this thought went through my mind:

We are all in lockdown, all the time. We just don't know it, that's all.

But we do the best we can. Most of us are just trying to get through.

. . .

A man walked by, scowling slightly above his mask, busy in his thoughts. There were window boxes across the street with lots of green and the bright yellow of pansies. A few cars went by on the street.

And then a gray car pulled up and William stepped out. He had his brown rolling little suitcase with him. I stood up and held out my arms. "Oh William," I said. We kept standing there embracing, we two old people on the sidewalks of New York, where we had arrived together so many, many years before.

"Closer," I said. "Closer."

And William pulled back for a moment and said "If I hold you any closer, I'll be behind you" before hugging me again; I could feel his arms encircling me. Then he said quietly, "I love you, Lucy Barton, for whatever it's worth."

A tiny shiver of foreboding passed through me then, a shiver of foreboding for myself and also the entire world. And I stood there holding on to this man as though he were the very last person left on this sweet sad place that we call Earth.

ACKNOWLEDGMENTS

I would like to acknowledge the following people who helped me bring this book to fruition: First and always, Kathy Chamberlain, my first reader. Also, my editor, Andy Ward; my publisher, Gina Centrello; my entire team at Random House; Molly Friedrich and Lucy Carson, Carol Lenna, Trish Riley, Pat Ryan, Beverly Gologorsky, Jeannie Crocker, Ellen Crosby, my daughter, Zarina Shea, and the wonderful Benjamin Dreyer.

MY NAME IS LUCY BARTON
ELIZABETH STROUT

Lucy is recovering from an operation in a New York hospital when she wakes to find her estranged mother sitting by her bed. They have not seen each other in years. As they talk, Lucy finds herself recalling her troubled rural childhood, and how it was she eventually arrived in the big city, got married and had children. But this unexpected visit leaves her doubting the life she's made: wondering what is lost and what has yet to be found.

'So good it gave me goosebumps. One of the best writers in America'

Sunday Times

'This is a glorious novel . . . deft, tender and true. Read it'

Sunday Telegraph

'An exquisite novel . . . in its careful words and vibrating silences, *My Name is Lucy Barton* offers us a rare wealth of emotion, from darkest suffering to – "I was so happy. Oh, I was happy" – simple joy'

Claire Messud, *New York Times Book Review*

ANYTHING IS POSSIBLE
ELIZABETH STROUT

Anything is Possible tells the story of the inhabitants of rural, dusty Amgash, Illinois, the hometown of Lucy Barton, a successful New York writer who finally returns, after seventeen years of absence, to visit the siblings she left behind.

Reverberating with the deep bonds of family, and the hope that comes with reconciliation, *Anything is Possible* again underscores Elizabeth Strout's place as one of America's most respected and cherished authors.

'This book, this writer, are magnificent'

Ann Patchett

'This is a shimmering masterpiece of a book . . . Strout is a brilliant chronicler of the ambiguity and delicacy of the human condition. *Anything is Possible* is a wise, stunning novel'

Observer

'*Anything is Possible* is absolutely wonderful. Here is a writer at the peak of her powers: compassionate, profoundly observant, laser-cut-diamond brilliant'

Literary Review

OH WILLIAM!
ELIZABETH STROUT

Lucy Barton is a successful writer living in New York, navigating the second half of her life as a recent widow and parent to two adult daughters. A surprise encounter leads her to reconnect with William, her first husband – and long-time, on-again-off-again friend and confidante. Recalling their college years, the birth of their daughters, the painful dissolution of their marriage, and the lives they built with other people, Strout weaves a portrait, stunning in its subtlety, of a decades-long partnership.

Oh William! is a luminous novel about the myriad mysteries that make up a marriage, about discovering family secrets, late in life, that rearrange everything we think we know about those closest to us, and the way people continue to live and love, against all odds. At the heart of this story is the unforgettable, indomitable voice of Lucy Barton, who once again offers a profound, lasting reflection on the mystery of existence. *'This is the way of life,'* Lucy says. *'The many things we do not know until it is too late.'*

'Devastating and vital'

Sunday Times

'Greatness'

Jennifer Egan

'A miraculous achievement'

Ann Patchett

He just wanted a decent book to read ...

Not too much to ask, is it? It was in 1935 when Allen Lane, Managing Director of Bodley Head Publishers, stood on a platform at Exeter railway station looking for something good to read on his journey back to London. His choice was limited to popular magazines and poor-quality paperbacks – the same choice faced every day by the vast majority of readers, few of whom could afford hardbacks. Lane's disappointment and subsequent anger at the range of books generally available led him to found a company – and change the world.

'We believed in the existence in this country of a vast reading public for intelligent books at a low price, and staked everything on it'
Sir Allen Lane, 1902–1970, founder of Penguin Books

The quality paperback had arrived – and not just in bookshops. Lane was adamant that his Penguins should appear in chain stores and tobacconists, and should cost no more than a packet of cigarettes.

Reading habits (and cigarette prices) have changed since 1935, but Penguin still believes in publishing the best books for everybody to enjoy. We still believe that good design costs no more than bad design, and we still believe that quality books published passionately and responsibly make the world a better place.

So wherever you see the little bird – whether it's on a piece of prize-winning literary fiction or a celebrity autobiography, political tour de force or historical masterpiece, a serial-killer thriller, reference book, world classic or a piece of pure escapism – you can bet that it represents the very best that the genre has to offer.

Whatever you like to read – trust Penguin.